Love is
a time of enchantment:
in it all days are fair and all fields
green. Youth is blest by it,
old age made benign:
the eyes of love see
roses blooming in December,
and sunshine through rain. Verily
is the time of true-love
a time of enchantment — and
Oh! how eager is woman
to be bewitched!

THE SWIFTEST EAGLE

This book moves from Scotland to Malaya — before British Raj and now — and then to war-torn Vietnam and Cambodia . . . Virginia meets Gareth casually in the Western Isles, with no inkling of the sacrifice he must make for her. Maybe Rat Fergusson steals the whole story in his old paddle steamer, the *Queen Victoria*, as he sails down the Mekong River, across the delta and out on the China Seas — with inflammable cargo. But Gareth Grant keeps his promise. He flies like the swiftest eagle . . .

Books by Alice Dwyer-Joyce
Published by The House of Ulverscroft:

THE MOONLIT WAY
THE DIAMOND CAGE
THE GINGERBREAD HOUSE
THE BANSHEE TIDE
FOR I HAVE LIVED TODAY
THE STROLLING PLAYERS
PRESCRIPTION FOR MELISSA
DANNY BOY
THE GLITTER-DUST
DOCTOR ROSS OF HARTON
THE STORM OF WRATH
THE PENNY BOX
THE RAINBOW GLASS
CRY THE SOFT RAIN

ALICE DWYER-JOYCE

THE SWIFTEST EAGLE

Complete and Unabridged

ULVERSCROFT
Leicester

First published in Great Britain in 1979 by
Robert Hale Limited
London

First Large Print Edition
published 1997
by arrangement with
Robert Hale Limited

E493210

British Library CIP Data

Dwyer-Joyce, Alice
    The swiftest eagle.—Large print ed.—
Ulverscroft large print series: romance
1. English fiction—20th century
2. Large type books
I. Title
823.9′14 [F]

ISBN 0–7089–3700–4

Published by
F. A. Thorpe (Publishing) Ltd.
Anstey, Leicestershire
Set by Words & Graphics Ltd.
Anstey, Leicestershire
Printed and bound in Great Britain by
T. J. Press (Padstow) Ltd., Padstow, Cornwall

This book is printed on acid-free paper

I dedicate this book
to the little families,
that sailed the China Seas
in cockle-shell boats
seeking for home

Author's Note

In this novel Frazer was known as 'The Little Hopper' and Menzies was called 'Gordonstoun'.

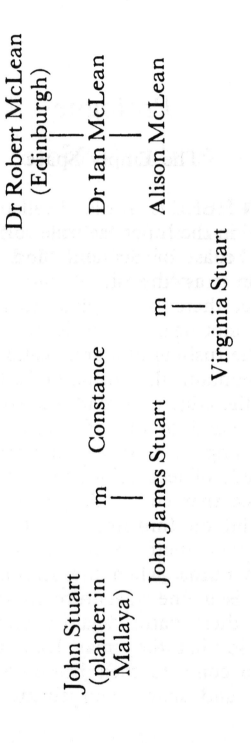

Prologue

The Empty Space

THERE is an island called Turnish in the Inner Hebrides off the west coast of Scotland and I always look on it as 'the isle of running water'. To me, there is no place there, where one cannot hear the music of the waters, be it the rushing of a great cataract down the mountain, the gushing of a tiny burn along the edge of a road, the song of the sea, tranquil or full of wrath, the crash of the long fall into the deep brown pool hundreds of feet below. Over everything is peace that comes dropping as slowly as it did on Innisfree . . . If you crave excitement, there are the salmon coming up the burns, when the season is right and it is a fine adventure to stand and watch their battle against unspeakable odds, so that they may leap weir after weir to come to their breeding grounds at last and spawn and ensure that the seas and the waters will be fruitful and replenish the earth . . . ensure that in hundreds of years, there will be salmon, so that one can stand on a Highland bridge and watch them packed as tightly in the clear water below, as maybe sardines will still be packed into tins, but that's civilisation for you and has no part in this story.

You come to Turnish on the fine new ferry nowadays and your car can travel with you. You drive on at the mainland port and off at the Turnish landing stage and there will be people waiting and perhaps a bus that has seen better days. This is an event of the week and there will be a small crowd down on the quay with no intention to travel anywhere. The bus passengers will be country folk come in to town to do the messages or maybe to leave a pair of fowl, legs tied together, ordered a week in advance, a basket of eggs, butter freshly-churned. It's an important day indeed, when a salmon is put aboard the boat on its way back to the mainland and an old seaman takes his pipe from between his teeth and says drily that 'maybe the exports from the

Island are going up and that may please the folk in Lunnon.'

After the boat has gone, there is no hurry for the bus to set out on its way back along the length of the island. When everybody is ready, that is the time for the bus to leave. Now instead of eggs and butter and the produce of the islands, we have the shopping from civilisation . . . the cans of baked beans, the packet of tea, the salt and the pepper and the cloves . . . the cinnamon, the rice, dear God, the rice!

The road starts off well enough but after a while, it narrows, so that there is not room for two cars abreast. There are small bays, where one vehicle awaits the pleasure of the other and there is no hurry, only a great inborn courtesy, anyway time was made for slaves and if freedom is anywhere, it is here . . . and soon there is a line of grass that grows along the road centre and all around is beauty. On a clear day, there are the mountains and the wind chasing the shadows across them, turning them to rose to blue, to all the colours of spectrum grace. The sea is to our right hand, as blue or as green as the weather wishes . . . and the hazel-nut groves and the lichened walls and the small grey-stone crofts, with the shining windows and the net curtains impossibly white and the flock of fowl, that runs across expectantly to meet the bus . . . the guard dog, that barks in friendship, against the hope of a bone brought from the butcher's.

There is a pause at each cottage and maybe some gossip. The District Nurse has been on her rounds and it is small wonder that 'Morag is showing her size already'. The older women on the bus are not meeting your eye at the way the young ones talk nowadays about such matters in public and no shame on them.

I often ride on the bus from the port, just for the fun of it, for the simplicity of it and for the return to basic things. I know well that my heart will beat faster presently, when we come near the Island of Slievenailra. It stands well off shore, but is not truly an island. At low tide, one can walk to it dry shod across a granite causeway and there is a castle set on the side of a mountain and here is 'the Mountain of the Eagles'. Sometimes you can see an eagle hover high against the sky. If you watch him, maybe, he may come plummeting, like a thunderbolt, as the poem says. Then up he goes and away to his spartan nest and you know that there will be eaglets there with their beaks open for food. He is a noble bird and I love the legend that the eagles leave this very special mountain, when the Laird leaves the castle . . . return, only when he returns and this legend, is true, to my own knowledge. I have a very special interest in the Castle on Slievenailra on Turnish . . . a vested interest, that the eagles will stay there down many generations to come and that this island will not know the bitterness of wars nor the rumours of wars, but only the wind in the heather and the rowan berries on the tree and the kindness of one neighbour to another . . . that it may always be the most important thing on Turnish, whether Morag McLean or any of the mothers that come after her, will be due to produce one child or two, for that is the stuff the world turns on.

Number One Son, we called him that day but I looked on down the years. Number Two Son would be no less important. For all sons were equal in the eyes of the true God, but there were so many gods . . .

I shall never forget Slievenailra Castle, but I knew of it long before I came to it. There was this grassy track that led steeply up from the main road, where the bus went. Even the main road grew grass down the middle, but the track to the Castle was a sheep track and it needed the land rover in the winter on the wet days and the snowy days. The track shot you out on a horizontal ledge of the mountain and here was a lawn, or what passed as a lawn, but it was hungry sea grass, yet when the time was right, there were cowslips growing there or primroses, or tiny exquisite orchids, that reminded me of places on the other side of the world. The castle was Rapunzel style and there was a tower, where Rapunzel might have let down her hair. Here was the bastion of a Scottish castle, with high towers and leaded battlements . . . There was a look about it of a castle on the

6

Rhine, but the magic was hard, not soft. Here was a fortress to hold till death. Maybe this clan of eagles did just that. Yet there was romance about it and a softness and a long history, a history of integrity and loyalty and of the years and the years, that had gone by, flowing under the bridge in the water below, for you could draw up a portcullis at low tide and be inviolable.

Somebody had built the kirk at the side of the orchid-strewn grass. It was a family place, a grey-walled church with stained glass windows . . . with a central aisle and with an aisle either side and a humble altar . . . the usual oblong brass catalogue of the names of the dead fallen in two world wars, the brass plates, that glorified the men of Turnish, who had given their lives in the cause of the British Empire, that it might be free.

The Laird's family went back down the years. They had served gallantly in every theatre of war. Some of them had died, venerable old men and women in the service of their people.

It was a way of passing a boring sermon to study the brightly shining brass plates, that commemorated every laird and his wife and his children and his children's children. Here was family history, cut out in brass for all to read.

We occupied a box pew in the front of the kirk, as befitted the people who lived in the castle and the Laird sat at the seat by the aisle, and presently he would read the lesson, but for now, his mind was occupied by the person he called 'Number One Son'.

I turned my eyes back to the kirk wall and came to the space, that always halted me and spun me back down the years. God only knows why we had never made the wall good. It would have been a simple matter to plaster up the small holes, that the screws had made. Along the wall, were the family plaques and those of retainers too, but all of the Clan. There was no space unfilled, only right beside where I sat near the inner aisle, there was this blank gap, maybe a yard by eighteen inches, where there had been a brass plate displayed in pride and I knew what had been written upon it, just as well as the Laird himself knew. It told of a soldier, dead in battle, but it was one of the modern battles and God knows he had been no soldier, yet the bravest of them all. They had taken down his memorial and perhaps I was the only person in the kirk that Sabbath Day, who knew the whole story.

Always my eyes went back to the empty space and the wall fading where the brass plate had hidden it. I had just but to close my eyes and remember that worst day of them all. It had been raining in that quick tropical downpour and we had been soaked to the skin. Then the rain had stopped and we were dry as the desert again. I was leading the donkey and Jenny was riding on it and the nuns had been right. Before long, her baby would be born and I thought back to the delivery rooms I had known, where one had but to reach out a hand for all the accessories of modern birth. I had been envisaging the packs, which contained the whole equipment for a maternity case, neatly ready and proof against contamination, the hundred and one things, without which one can not deliver a baby. I was going to have to deliver a child soon and I tried to think

9

of one asset we possessed between us. I might tear clothes into strips but they were strip-torn already. The burner had not been working for two days. The children were bitten by mosquitoes and they were fretful. The excitement had all worn off. There was such a long long way to go.

Only for the donkey, we would never have got even as far as we had managed to come. The lost goat had arrived in the back of a jeep. I had secured her with my belt as a lead, but she had eaten that and yet without any lead, she had kept company with us, for she was outcast too . . . but that was not yet. The sun was cruel and the tropical day burnt us up and our sandals were scuffed to uselessness and our spirits low. Always the thought of Jenny and her baby tortured me. There was nothing in this awful place and nothing in my knowledge of midwifery to prepare me for this, yet the nuns had trusted me. The dog licked my hand. He had joined us somewhere along the way and he was a flea-bitten lurcher with countable ribs, but he caught food for us. Suzy and I had cooked it crudely over open fires and we had eaten it half raw, but I could not go on much longer. I had an idea that I had a fever of some kind. Last night I had thought I was in the Holy Land, but this was a most unholy land. I had thought it was Christmas night and that the shepherds were minding their sheep. I had thought the whole world was waiting tiptoe for the coming of Christmas Day and now I went staggering on across the arid plain and then there was the sound of a car engine, that stuttered and died and a man's voice said that maybe he had run out of petrol and blast it, but it was probably just a plug. He was in the jeep and he, wearing tattered slacks and a bright shirt. There was a straw hat tilted over his eyes and he did not seem to care, whether he had run out of transport or not. He smiled at me, as I stood at the donkey's head and then his glance took in Jenny and Suzy and ran along the small woebegone faces.

"Hello there, Holy Family," he said. "Are you really there, or are you some sort of a mirage?"

I had come to, to find myself on the

ground and his arm about me. He had fetched water from somewhere and he was moistening my lips.

"I thought you were a boy," he said and laughed. "But now I see you're not. Are you the leader of this . . . expedition and what's your name?"

"My name is Virginia," I said.

"Virginia Stuart," he had said. "Of course it is. Are you haunting my life?"

That is the point when my mind always switches back to the present day . . . when I knew it was all past and best forgotten.

If I had it to do all over again, I would have played it out the same way. There was no getting away from what was past and over, but sometimes, in the night, I remember all that happened and think that I have a debt to pay that I can in no way repay, did I live for a hundred years and more besides, but maybe I shall repay it down the years of eternity, for I found something very valuable . . . something without price . . . something immortal.

1

The Malayan Peninsula

I PICKED up volume seven of *Everyman's Encyclopaedia*, the other day, the fourth edition, published in 1958, INC-LIN, and the page fell open at Kuala Lumpur, cap. of the Malay State of Selangor, nearly opposite Port Swettenham on the w. coast of the Malay Peninsula and the heart of the Malayan rubber and tin-mining industries. With a good water supply and lit by electricity, it was remarkable before the Second World War for its easy, opulent way of life, due to the prosperity of the rubber and the tin companies. The native quarters are within the city; the residential areas, where officials and business men live, in the outskirts. In these areas, are spacious houses, with marvellous gardens, where cannas and hibiscus shrubs bloom in profusion. When Kuala Lumpur fell to the Jap. invaders in Jan. 1942, the city

13

presented a tragic spectacle . . .

I did not have to read about it. Since the first day I remember, I had heard all about it. I had not even been thought of in 1942, but in some strange way, I have been caught up with Malaya all my life and with the China Seas and the Gulf of Siam and with Vietnam and with Cambodia, though the names are changed and the rulers too. The British Raj has moved into history. There are other rules and other rulers and Cambodia is the Khmer Republic and Saigon is Ho Chi Minh city and Singapore is a State in its own right, but the frogs still croak in the paddy fields and at night, the cicadas sing and the fireflies flit among the trees in the villages, and a dog barks against the stranger.

My grandfather, John Stuart, was a rubber planter in Malaya, on a large estate to the north of Kuala Lumpur. He lived with his wife, Constance, in one of these luxurious, spacious houses, the Encyclopaedia describe, with a marvellous garden . . . cannas, hibiscus bushes and all. There was a swimming pool and a tennis court and a host of Malayan servants and Chinese too. Perhaps, there was little in the way of gracious living, that might not have been theirs . . .

Constance Stuart was a good Scots housewife and I imagine she was less easy-going, less pleasure-loving than the ordinary planter's wife. For some reason, when I look back over the story of my grandparents, I always think of John Anderson, my jo, John, of whom Robbie Burns wrote. 'They clamb the hill te gither' and 'many a cantie day,' as he puts it, 'we've had wi' ane anither.'

They had been in Malaya for many years. In 1939, the second world war broke out, but to most people on the Peninsula, it was a phony war. There was a social round, no different from usual, not that Constance or John cared much for dances and tennis parties and bridge sessions. My father was their only son and he had been home a few years from his English school. The war was unreal in that lovely bungalow. The power of the British Raj was a fortress, against which the Germans would break. They lived the same life, watched cricket in

Kuala Lumpur, at the club, attended church every Sunday and life went on. Uniforms began to appear in the capital and my father had joined the Navy and was away . . . and the Stuarts knew that the war was not phony after all. Then came the day of Pearl Harbour and the Japanese were at war and Constance might murmur that it was 'a gey fine thing to have America on the side of the Empire', but the sinking of the Prince of Wales and the Repulse must have been a cold wind through her heart.

John, my father, now Lieutenant Commander Stuart, was safe in a naval base in the Hebridean Islands off the West coast of Scotland. It seemed a good safe distance from Japan, or so I imagine, Constance might have thought, yet ships were being sunk in increasing numbers. Then suddenly, the danger was not far away. The Japs might have seemed of small importance for a while, it was impossible to believe that they had landed in Malaya. They were fighting in a manner, that could not be understood by traditional soldiers — fighting as no man had fought before. They spread like a forest fire, but a letter had come to the bungalow, weeks late from John James. It seemed that he had met the girl he wanted to marry. I always think of Constance, standing in the bright light of the garden, where she had gone to find my grandfather.

"But he's only a laddie and he says she's a Queen Wren and he met her in some base in Argyll . . . says she's a smasher."

She was reluctant to marry him, till the war was over, but time moved as fast for them as the Jap soldiers moved up the Malayan Peninsula. He had been posted abroad and she had been sent to a base in the south . . .

I know now that he was commanding a destroyer in the Battle of the Atlantic and that she was stationed in Portsmouth, but letters had the safety of anonymity then. . . . They had thought that they might never meet again. They had found a greystone kirk on the side of a Scots hill.

'At least, we have today and they can't take that away from us.'

'She is just such a girl, as you must have been, Mother — very practical and beautiful with it. She has the heart of a lioness and hair, snow-white for all her youth. They call it ash-blond nowadays . . . oh, and her name is Alison McLean, and she's the only daughter of a doctor in Edinburgh, where all good doctors are manufactured and he approves of me, for he's R.N.V.R. but being a doctor, he has a red stripe between the gold ones on his cuff . . . '

'God keep you safe, both of you, keep you in the hollow of His hand, till we meet again. After this cauldron of nations has gone off the boil . . . the four of us can drive into Kuala Lumpur and show Alison off to the Club and go across to watch the cricket and sit in cane loungers and drink iced drinks and talk and talk and talk of all that has happened and is going to happen . . . '

There was a P.S. He had enclosed two locks of hair, his and hers, because he knew that Grandmother liked such old-fashioned customs.

I have the letter still. It was found in my grandparents' effects, all that was left of the lifetime they spent, climbing the hill together. The envelope is yellow with age, or perhaps the smoke did it, but the two locks of hair still live, Mother's hair as white as a moonbeam and Father's as black as a raven and that is how I remembered them in life.

My grandfather must have put the letter into the safe, after he told Constance the other news, that had come with the post. Kuala Lumpur was to be evacuated and all the surrounding countryside. The women and children were to go first and then was to come the 'burnt earth policy'. The tin-mines were to be blown up and the plantations burnt, the homes destroyed utterly — the paddy fields were to be ruined and all buildings must go. The land was to be laid waste . . .

How can there be any account of what happened on that plantation? My father went there after the war and got the story from a Chinese, who had been head cook. He had waited in the ruins and like all his race, he was patient. He bent his head, as he put it, and let the fire storm of the Japanese sweep over him, and when they were gone, he stood up straight again. He lived in a house on stilts, when my father found him and he had pigs that lived under the house and fowls in the yard. He took two crops of rice a year from his paddy fields and was on his way to being a prosperous man and he was happy.

My father did not hurry the story out of him. They talked about the change in the country and how strange it was that time went so fast. The days had been good, when the Memsahib had come into his kitchen, to show him how to make Scottish shortbread . . . and how pleased she had been with him, but it was all water, that had gone down the river and the Memsahib was with her ancestors.

It had taken so long to tell and my father was very unhappy. He knew some of it, but not the small details, that threw him.

All the memsahibs had gone and all the little ones, but there was no place to go. The railway was crowded with troops, moving up. There was no petrol and no tyres and cars were left along the roads. There was nothing but the great star of the British Raj, falling down the sky. The prisoners of war were pitiful. It was a terrible thing to see a great Tuan brought low, but with the Japanese, it was a dishonour for a soldier to be taken alive in battle and not to die, so the British prisoners were given no honour. It was all bitter history. My father turned back the focus on the bungalow, where Constance had taught a Chinese to make Scots shortbread.

'The Memsahib did not go.'

She had stayed by 'John Anderson, my jo, John.' The sky was filled with rolling columns of smoke and the air full of soot sparks. All about them, there were fires burning as so many years of work destroyed. At intervals, the whole earth shook with the detonation of one mined bridge after another. The birds in the trees were silent. There must be no bridge left and no way out any more, but the Memsahib was not frightened. Some of the Malayans had run off when the Tuan told them to go, but the Chinese had stayed and Constance had asked him to make tea. The bungalow must be burnt as all the rest of Malaya was being burnt, but 'there was time for a cup of tea and some of my small sugar cakes'.

It was all so ordinary, nothing dramatic about it. 'The floor was highly polished and as she came to thank me for being such a trusted friend, she slipped and fell. Her head hit the low table and it was a good thing for her, for she went quickly to her God.' That was what the old man said. Her head was against the side of the little table and not quite straight. Some of the servants had come back. They wept for her — Tamil and Malayan and Indian — my humble self. We made a grave where the Tuan showed us and he put a cross at the head of it. Then he said we must go, for the small yellow men were almost in the plantation and it was time for fire. He threw petrol about the house and the trees were already torches against the sky. We crept back in the shadows, but he did not watch us go. He took a blossom from the hibiscus and he put it on the grave and he had a gun in his hand and he sat down on the edge of the fountain and by the strange will of the white God, the fountain was throwing up graceful jets of water still in all the fire, that was burning up the British Raj . . . '

'He waited for them and many times we stole back and begged him to come into the shadows to hide, but he would not leave the Memsahib's grave, till the Japanese with their guns wrote finish across his chest. In the night, we came, for their soldiers did not harm us. We dug another grave by hers, so that they would be happy.'

That was the legend of my grandparents. My father and mother survived the war and eventually they were demobbed and it seemed that England was not a bright and glorious land any more. There was a shortage of food and a shortage of work. It was a lucky break, when the Company, who had employed my grandfather, sought them out. My father had been brought up in Malaya. He spoke Malayan and Chinese like a native. He was ex-R.N. and so was she.

Such a couple as John James Stuart and Alison was on the priority list.

They were flown out to Malaya to a position in the British government to try to rehabilitate the interests of the rubber industry and tin mining and rice. There was a peace to be won too and a future to be built.

What interest is there in politics? I was to be born in 1952 and nothing was more interesting to me than myself.

See me then, Virginia, the only daughter of John James and Alison McLean Stuart, growing up in a house well to the north of Kuala Lumpur with a Chinese Amah, who saw that I was unspoilt and who was called Suzy Chan. I can recall her, down to the last starched stitch in the short white jacket with the slits up the sides and the high collar and the black cotton trousers and the wide cool round straw hat.

"It is no good saying that it is too hot for Missie to do her sums. It is a good thing to know that two and two are not five and to know it, with no abacus in her hand. When Missie grows up, no man will look at her, if she cannot count . . . and a hand is a good thing too for a correction slap . . . and it is no use either to ask God to make your hair go from white to black. My hair is black because my mother's hair was black . . . my grandmother's hair

24

was black, when she was a young girl. The lady, your mother, has hair, like the moon shining and it does not mean that she is old woman. You can burn a joss stick in the snake temple in Penang for a million years and your hair will still not be different. You should give thanks that people turn in the street to look at you, for perhaps they think you are an angel, but they are not knowing you, as I know you."

The maid, who did the cooking, was Malayan, and she was gentler than my Amah, Suzy Chan. She baked the little cakes I liked and cooked the shrimps with rice, that were my favourite dish. She could fluff up eggs into an omelette to coax my capricious appetite. She taught me to speak Malay. Suzy and I chattered away in Mandarin Chinese too and when my parents were present, we spoke good Scots English, so I was a polyglot, by the time I was six. It was easy enough for me. Malaya was a country of all nations, Indian, Pakistani, Malays, Chinese and the last of the British Raj. Canadians, Australians, Scots, English, Welsh. We did not leave the plantation much. Father and Mother preferred to stay at home. A few times a week, they had to take the Land Rover into Kuala Lumpur to do government work and to attend conferences and committees, but they were home birds as my grandparents had been.

There were plenty of children to play with, children of other government officials and the children of the 'servants' too, for they were 'servants' no longer, but counted as an equal to any white child, for was it not their country now and ours no longer? At least, that's how Father explained it to me.

Anyhow, we had a wonderful time and I liked the Malayans better than any other race, for they were gentle and kind and they did not like to work any more than I did. My mother said they took after the English in that they preferred good manners to getting on in life, but I did not know what she meant by that, though maybe she was right. It was one of her jobs to encourage the Malayans to produce more rice, but if God had willed them to produce one crop a year, that was all right by them. My mother had to sell them the idea of two crops, even if it meant pedalling water up from the river all day with a bicycle contraption and there was no fun in that. I could see the Malayan point of view better than Mother could. She could drive the Land Rover through the bright streets of Kuala Lumpur any time she liked. She could go round Singapore and Malacca and Penang and circle Penang Island on tours of inspection, but she homed to our bright bungalow like a pigeon and stayed there every hour she could spare and I loved her beyond the whole world. Her hair might be white, but the first time I read 'she walks in beauty like the night', I thought that was just what she did. Alison McLean Stuart, she was, the daughter of a doctor from Edinburgh. He, of course, was my maternal grandfather and I kept up an extraordinary correspondence with him. He had been demobbed from the Royal Navy Volunteer Reserve and he had a General Practice in a place in the Highlands. It was I, who started writing letters to him, though at the time, I cannot have had much control of written English. He replied in block capitals, illustrated with small line-drawings and for a long time, I thought that 'red-letter days', were the days, they arrived in Malaya. *Dr Ian McLean*, I would address my replies, *The Surgery, Glenmore, Argyll, Scotland. The United Kingdom* and think it was by some strange magic that a man, he called 'the postie', would walk 'up the brae' with my letters. In years to come, when I was a doctor myself, we were to laugh over them, but by then, I was ready to take over the healing of the whole world, fresh from the Royal College, and maybe with not so much learning in my head, as I thought.

Just for now, I was eight years old and soon for a Scots Boarding School for girls. It was near enough to Glenmore for me to spend the weekends with Grandfather McLean and I could hardly wait to meet him. In addition, I had been reading school stories and if this type of literature is not a confidence trick as bad as Father Christmas, then nothing is. They still go in for 'japes in the dorm' and 'midnight feasts' and of course, there are all the new clothes and the trunk and the tuck box. God help me! I was taken in too. I could hardly wait to get up the gangway to the plane. There was nothing to fear. Suzy Chan was to come with me and lodge at Glenmore. Suzy had no family and my mother knew well that she would be just as lost without me, as I would be without her.

For the last three years, I had attended a day school a few miles from the bungalow. It was supposed to be very exclusive and we wore light blue cotton uniforms and white ankle socks. We were an extraordinary mixture of nations . . . Malayans, Chinese, Indians, Israelis, Canadians, United Kingdom. The nuns, who taught us, were Irish and a big proportion of us, including myself, thought that these nuns had discovered Christ and that Ireland was the centre of the civilised world, yet I was inclined to be faithful to Confucius, for I had a Chinese period in my life. Still I was starting to try to find out about Aesculapius, for I was thinking of taking up the profession of healing. I had been sounding out Grandfather

McLean in my letters but I had not got much useful information so far, though our letters were more mature by the time I was eight than the first day I wrote to him, aged three.

My heart thudded with excitement, when the time came to load the Land Rover with my new trunk and my tuck box and with a hockey stick and a tennis racket. Suzy Chan was wearing her best white starched jacket, her best black cotton trousers and a round wide straw hat. She had thonged sandals on her bare feet and she was obstinate enough not to take advice about the climate in foreign parts. That was what a good class amah of Malaya always wore and she was not going to bring loss of face to the Tuan's family by landing in Scotland dressed like the 'guy' on the feast of November the fifth, when even the white people let off fire-works.

I was excited at the thought of the adventure to come. I was longing to get away from home and I was already planning a feast in the dorm on the first convenient midnight. I was planning to be Head Girl of the School and the Captain of the Cricket Team. I hoped that my polyglot ability would make me an object of admiration. I had no suspicion that my knowledge of languages might make them consider me a 'poor wee lassie from outlandish parts', who had been forced to flee to Scotland to find proper food and fresh air. There were a few other immigrants like myself at St Mary Peter's. I did not think that much of a name for a school, but by the time I left it, I classified it with pride in the ranks of Eton and Harrow, but female, of course, because it was run by the Holy Sisters.

"You'll get your death of cold, Suzy," my mother said as we drove through the outskirts of Kuala Lumpur. "I've packed leather boots and warm jumpers and good wool underclothes for you and of course wellingtons. You'll see why, when you get out of the plane in Scotland."

All the same, it had been a sobering thought to watch the day girls being collected from school in Malaya. Big glossy cars, chauffeur-driven, arrived to collect the Malayans, the Chinese, the people of Israel and most of the others.

Chinese amahs came for the UK girls, tucked them into rickshaws and they were pedalled off home by the rickshaw boys. It did not seem strange to me, but a great change had come about and nations had been gathered into the hand of fate and shaken up and cast out on the gaming table — and last might be first and first last and that all the UK held in Malaya was her great business interests and her nostalgia for the lost luxurious life — maybe too a relief at the knowledge that she was governess of the world no longer.

The time had passed very slowly till I could be away to Scotland. I succeeded in interesting Grandfather a little in helping me to become a doctor. I could repack his accident bag after it had been used on a night visit, he promised me. He drew one of his sketches of me with a slate on my head and a roll of paper in my hand. I already knew about the Snake Temple at Penang, where the priests were healers. When I look back down the years, I see the pattern of life and the extraordinary way it was woven right from the start.

"Och! what a portrait he's drawn of your wee self." Mother smiled. "And you with a mortar board on your head and your 'pairchment' in your hand, standing on the steps of the University, but mebbe I'll take you to the Snake Temple and get them to give you a few lessons in the art of packing emergency bags. Himself is a particular man, and you'd not want to make a mistake."

Mother was sad to see me go. She was pale under her sun-tan and Father was silent and very kind to me. I was too excited to worry about anything. I sat on the edge of my seat and looked out of the car window at the excitement, that was central Kuala Lumpur. The streets were full of bright new cars and the shops were sophisticated and smart.

The police had well-pressed shorts and smart jackets, and they might have been the lords of creation for the air of authority they had. The streets themselves might have been garlanded with flowers, for the Chinese girls had put on their cheongsams to come to town — gay sprightly pyjamas. The Malayan girls wore colourful sarongs to the ankle and perhaps a blouse of lace to cover the shoulders. The Indians were the best, so cool and graceful and beautiful in their silk saris. The caste mark on their foreheads was a thing of mystery and glamour. I was happy that day and there was no doubt that Kuala Lumpur was happy too.

"It's not like Indonesia," Father muttered to himself. "They've benefited from colonisation and de-colonisation too and they're on the way up, given half a chance. Three million Malays, two and a half million Chinese and three quarter of a million others . . . all in a peninsula the size of England without Wales!"

I did not take much notice of what he said. He was always quoting dull statistics and figures, of this and that.

We had shrimps with rice in a very splendid café, all glass and chromium. Then we had curry and sliced cucumber and coconut and all sorts of delicious things and afterwards, a tall ice cream with fruit on top and chopped nuts sprinkled all over. I was too excited to eat much and Suzy Chan ordered hardly anything. She murmured reproaches to me that it was a wicked thing for 'Missie' not to finish what was put before her. The day might come, when she would think back to this day and wish she had the wasted food.

She was threatening what was to come true, but there were many tears to flow under the bridge and down the river by then. Even in the Convent School, all the same, I realised, that Suzy was as wise as Confucius. It was on a day, when I ploughed my way, sick for home, through porridge and macaroni cheese and followed that up with lumpy white blancmange, and years after, there was a time when I would have been very glad of it indeed.

I had been foolish enough to insist on wearing my new school outfit, gym slip, white blouse, warm wool pants and long black stockings. I had been soaked in sweat after five minutes and my white blouse a rag, but I was too proud to admit my mistake.

"Honourable parents know best," Suzy Chan murmured. "It is right to learn by experience."

My father retreated into silence as the

time drew on. On holidays in the years to come, I too, was to be silent at the parting, but today, my excitement blotted out the white under the sun-tan in their faces. I took to the air like a bird and no look over my shoulder. I intended to get full value.

I got full value at every stop, looked at the shops, that sold goods for export, tried out exotic drinks on the plane, ate my way through every course of food carried across half the world and refused to admit to myself that it was anything so good as what we had at home in the bungalow. I slept for a while and then woke up, with no idea of where I was, except that there were thousands of feet between myself and the earth and knew a small panic, but was not Suzy with me and she had no fear? She had taken off her straw hat and the air conditioning suited her to perfection. She was sweetly pretty in her white jacket and there was no wrinkle or crease in it. Her hair was black as night and smooth against her head and the graceful little fringe just reached the slanting brows. Her eyes were deep and black and she had a face like a small hungry cat, her head slightly on one side, her body like a boy's, her hands folded calmly in her lap. We looked at a chinese film, and then Suzy was leaning to me.

"The worst is over now and honourable parents will be getting used to Missie not being at home, only the house will be very empty for a few days."

She smiled at me and asked me, if I wished more rice with shrimps, for I might not see them in Scotland and soon the plane might be dropping us down in this strange foreign country.

It was all over in the time it might take to go home from Kuala Lumpur to the bungalow, or so it seemed. Now we were coming in to land and I was putting on the gaberdine coat and tidying my hair, setting the school hat on my head, a bit tilted over my nose to give me style . . . all ready to take the western world in fee.

There was a wind with a razor edge to it, that met us as we disembarked. Suzy Chan seemed to shrink into herself, as we hurried to the shelter of the Customs. Her straw hat was the most impossible wear for such weather, not to mention the cotton trousers and the cold starch of the tunic, but I was selfish enough to have no worry on her behalf and we were through Customs quickly and out into the front hall. There were people there and I had to identify Grandfather and surely, he should have been looking for me? There was no one looking for anybody. Right enough, there was an enormous man, with a craggy face, wearing what I now know was an Inverness cape. He was standing over by a statue, that dominated the hall and he carried a strange tall walking stick like a staff, in his hand with a forked top to it for his thumb. I walked over and stood at his side and Suzy Chan stepped neatly a pace behind me. He never moved or turned to see if we were there. He knew already, with no turn to his head. He waved the stick at the statue and remarked that 'Yon was Robbie Burns'. Then he turned round and gripped my shoulder in his hand, till I winced. His whole face was lit with gladness, but there was a tear on his eye and I imagined he felt the cold.

"Now I have a prop to my whole house," he cried. "It's been weary passing the years against your coming, but now you're here and I'll not have to be watching for the postie every day to get a note from you."

It all happened at once, for he took Suzy Chan and saw how cold she was and at the same time a boy got out of a car at the entrance and came walking towards us. The boy was wearing the kilt and a warm overcoat and there was a long scarf wound round his throat again and again and still too much of it to make it reach a normal length, as I knew scarves.

"Slievenailra's boy," said the old man and reached out a hand to take his. "Is it on your way to school you are, like my wee lassie here? I daresay the old eagle has sent you in from the Isles for them to make a man of you at Gordonstoun? Does he no' ken that his father's son is a fine man born and that he has all the humanities, but will you tell me what's to do wi' this lassie here? She's petrified with the day and there's not even a rug in the car."

The boy was smiling and had his coat off in a trice. It was round Suzy's shoulders and then he had her straw hat in his hand and the scarf unwound from his neck. He wrapped it round her head and about her throat again and again and he made her an oriental little bow and said "Welcome to Scotland! You'll get used to it, but I don't know if I'll ever get used to being away from The Isles."

Then he was gone, coatless across to the place where the plane was waiting, his school cap tilted over his eyes, the kilt swinging bravely, yet I imagined he was almost as strange as myself and lonely for his home.

"That's the Eaglet and one day he'll be as fine a man as his father is today and mind Janet to send the coat after him and the scarf. I daresay she'll bake a Dundee cake for him too, for he'll miss the Eagle's fine castle and the way the women wait on his every wish. Och! Yon school mebbe will be the making of him." The Eagle's son was to remember the Dundee cake down a great many years and he was to recall it in a wild country in a far-off place. He was to be woven

40

into my destiny as the colours were into his scarf. He was to make a shelter for me against the cruelty of life, just as he did that very first day for Suzy Chan.

Just for now, there was the drive to Glenmore on a sunny day with a wind that was freshening into a storm. The clouds filled the sky and threw down their shadows to chase across the mountains and the colours turned, like semi-precious stone shades . . . blue to pink, to amber to green to sage to emerald and then back to shell . . . the palest shell. There were small streams, that coursed the road-sides and waterfalls, that sparkled clear from the edges of the hills and I thought what a fertile land it must be with water so abundant. The colours of Malaya were dramatic and exotic, but here all was gentleness, yet the mountains were wild and fierce. There were kestrels hovering and deer, that ran free against the sky line and once we saw cattle with horns a yard long. It was an empty land. Rarely did we meet another car. The road was any road to start with, but it dwindled down to another road and to another road and always narrower, they got. Soon there was a line of green grass in the centre and that showed how little they were used but I know jungle tracks. Then after a few hours we were climbing a great mountain to a pass and I thought I might be able to see the whole of Scotland from the top of it. Then down a small steep hill we ran, and round a serpent bend and right round again and again and again, till we came out on the sea and a scatter of houses.

"There's Glenmore for you — the end of the earth, Lassie. Welcome home!"

The waves, were lashing the bay, the rocky headlands and the white sands of the bay, waves that threatened to engulf all the small houses and wash them away. There were some small ships that bobbed up and down on the uneasy waters — and it was cold, cold, cold.

"The tide's running in from the Isles and there's a storm coming. Mebbe, Neptune wants to see why Slievenailra's son's been exiled . . . sent in to learn to mind his manners, no less. It's a wonder his mother didn't send him south to make a Sassenach of him, for all the sense she has in her head. He's a braw fine laddie and one day he'll be lord of every foot his eye can scan from the peak of Slievenailra . . . but do you see yon wee ships out there? Tonight, when the storm gets up strong, and the tide runs high, there'll be a man standing guard in every one of them. There's a change in the day. Och! Aye! Don't fret that the house won't stand fast against it. It's a fine strong house and it's weathered many a storm."

Janet, the house-keeper, had the door open for us and she shut out the elements with the stout oak. It was wonderful the way tranquillity and peace came round us like a warm shawl of safety. There was a peat fire in the grate and a fine tea set ready for us. I had heard of Selkirk bannocks, of fresh baps, of Sally Lunns, of Scots scones, with the butter running down your chin. Suzy Chan might frown at me to remember my politeness and not to stuff myself like a goose for the market, but the latch was off my tongue and I was talking to Grandfather and telling what a fine place it was 'at home'. Maybe I patronised him a little, but I loved him too and thought what a sad thing it was that he had to live alone in this empty cold little town, with only a Scots housekeeper to mind him and not the band of servants, we had on the Peninsula. At one stage, when I was high on buttered scones, I even confided the future to him, how I had come to learn many things . . . but mostly about healing the sick.

"There's a Temple in Penang, where they worship snakes. There was somebody called Aesculapius and I think it was in Greece a long time ago, you wrote about him in one letter. The priests of the Penang Snake Temple are healers. The followers of Aesculapius worshipped the snake too. We want healers in Malaya and maybe I might worship Aesculapius? I'm going to stay at school till I learn a great deal and then I'm going to go to the place you find out about healing. You said Edinburgh University, for that's where you went to worship Aesculapius. I don't know if you burn joss sticks in Scotland, but snakes never bite you unless you annoy them . . . I'm not afraid, if I have to go to the Snake Temple at Edinburgh University."

He looked at me, his face very serious. "Do you tell me?" he said. "Haven't you got the great knowledge in your head for a wee lassie, but you're so like your mother at the same age, that the heart turns over in my breast."

Then he laughed and said he thought I had a fine plan and he hoped that I would carry it through and it would not be his fault if I didn't.

"For a woman of the world, that's so well travelled, it's only a step to the University and you can take your degree there and no fear of snake bite and visit with me whiles. Then you can come back here to Mistress Janet and myself and comfort the last years of our old age and maybe I can throw the torch to you and let you take over the healing of the sick folk of Glenmore, for there's no finer fishing in the whole country than there is in the rivers round here . . . and as for the bay out yonder, the salmon trout would give themselves up, if they thought you were in need of a good breakfast, but it's in my head you'll carry the torch of Aesculapius back to the other side of the world."

I went out to stand on the shore with him later and my gaberdine augmented by a plaid rug round my shoulders. My hair blew free in the wind and the sea was salt on my lips. Janet had taken Mistress Suzy off upstairs to a hot bath 'to thaw the ice out of her bones' and Grandfather and I were alone and his arm round me. Out in the bay, true enough, there was a man in the well of each boat, with the spray breaking over him. In yellow oilskins, they might have been a 'wheen of spirits' to guard against Old Nick, or so Grandfather said. The waves were washing the end wall of our garden and the small cold rain scourged our faces, and there was an excitement, an exhilaration. I was glad I had come to this foreign land . . . glad that the future was laid out for my feet to tread. The tuck box and the school could hold no delight to equal this. I pitied my parents that they were still in Malaya and likely lonely for me, yet I felt a small twinge of loneliness too as I wondered if they were thinking of me . . . if they knew I was thinking of them. I was used to the warm winds of Malaya, but the wind here was

46

cold . . . cold . . . cold and I shivered a little so we went back into the parlour. Grandfather filled a pipe and got it going to his satisfaction, kicked at the fire with the toe of his shoe and twinkled the soot of the chimney-back with stars.

"My wife always called 'peat' turf. That's what they call it yonder in Ireland. She's dead this long while and the place has been lone without her. You'll never know how welcome that first wee letter of yours was for I was missing Alison, your mother. You'll never know how glad I was to see you walking out into the Customs today. I spied through the window and you were our daughter again and the same white hair. I knew you'd be sure to have all the plans for the future cut and dried, though mind you, yours are far more fanciful than your mother's ever were."

He smiled at me and made a great joke of it.

"I'll warn you tonight, the same as I warned her, and she laughed at me, as I have nae doubt you'll do — just not to forget what Robbie Burns said. It was in the poem about the mousie. You'll recall

Robbie had turned her nest ower wi' his plough and her home was in ruins?"

"I don't know what he said, but I'm sure Mr Burns was very sorry."

" 'The best laid schemes of mice and men gang aft agley, An' lea'e us nought but grief and pain for promised joy . . . ' That's what he said, but your mother's made her way fine . . . wed the man she fancied and they finished wi' war and they're building a fine peace and they got themselves a grand lassie. There's no cloud in their sky, as far as I can see, only maybe that you're a mite far away from Malaya now, but as often as we can find a way, Mistress Suzy and you can go back to foreign parts for your holidays, so don't get despairing and think you'll never see them any more. Aye! Alison McLean Stuart's a girl with the heart of a lion cub. She knows where she's going and she knows who's going with her . . . and it's all working out. It's all working out, the way she planned it, your mother."

I remembered the warm winds of the Peninsula and thought of the cold wind, that was blowing in from the bay and there was a chill up my spine suddenly, as if a goose had walked over my grave. Then I thought that Suzy would be very proud to be called Mistress Suzy, for 'Mistress Suzy Chan' had a fine ring to it. Grandfather sent me off to bed and he tucked in the blankets himself and was awkward for a moment. He got it out at last. Did I want to have him 'hear' my prayers for me, for when his daughter, my mother, was my age, he used to 'hear' hers? It was a long time, since anybody had heard my prayers, but I thanked him and said I would be mighty obliged if he did me the honour. He creaked down beside the bed and I managed to say the Lord's prayer. I dismissed some of the supplications that Suzy and I made unofficially to Confucius and Aesculapius . . . filled in with a version of 'Christopher Robin' and asked God to bless my parents and keep Suzy and Grandfather safe . . . and also to make me a good girl, knowing very well that I was nothing of the sort, because I deceived him, even if it was a kind thing to do. He got slowly to his feet, when I was finished and I turned my head into

49

the pillow, so that he would think that I had not seen the tears on his face, and so I fell asleep.

I hated school at first. The routine was always the same. Late on Sunday night, or very early indeed on Monday, Grandfather dropped me back there after the week-end. The school was a very grand place with shaven lawns and steps up to the front door, but after my first introduction there, I knew that girls went in by a side entrance, which was guarded by an avenging angel called the 'Portress' who had a face like a saint and this gave one a wrong idea of her. The school was all echoing passages and flights of bare polished stairs. We seemed to move in a continuous line of girls at change of class time, and if we met a Holy Sister on the stairs or in the hall or in any of the passages, the moving belt of us came to a respectful halt. We did the same respectful halt for a sixth form girl and Suzy was very enthusiastic about this and many of the other rules.

If you wanted anything at the refectory table where you sat, you must never ask for it outright. You must watch everybody's plate and when they wanted something, you must offer it. It was all very good for 'face' to Suzy's way of thinking and now that I am older, I agree with her. Also, there was this strict question of honour. It was a disgrace here if you cheated. It had been quite the in thing to 'cog' and tell lies and break the rules in my blue cotton-dress-and-white-ankle-sock school. It was considered rather smart. Here, you would be taken aside by one of the big girls and probably nobody would talk to you all day, because you 'had let St Mary Peter's down'.

I fell in with it easily enough and I had no trouble with my lessons. I was sick for home for a long time and evenings in chapel at benediction were very hard on my emotions. If I started to cry, I might never leave off, so I managed not to, although, the gallery, where the new girls sat, was rather damp, as to handkerchief, pink as to eyes. There was plenty of sniffs at the more familiar prayers. When I felt really quite in despair, I would move my thoughts back to well before Christ and try Aesculapius, god of the medical art. I had looked him up in the school encyclopaedia. I knew that Homer called him 'the blameless physician.' My personal prayers with any god were very unorthodox, only excepting those I said with Grandfather.

"Aesculapius, please let me do my lessons well and get to Edinburgh or the Penang Snake Temple. I'd like it fine to be a good doctor and I don't mind snakes. There are lots of snakes in Malaya. I come from there."

On Friday night or early Saturday morning, Grandfather would collect me, or if he happened to be busy, I went by bus and Suzy Chan . . . 'Mistress Suzy', would walk along the road to meet the bus. She had settled in at Glenmore and was making herself useful to Janet. Janet liked her and treated her rather like a pretty Chinese doll, babied her a little — did not recognise the greatness, that was 'Mistress Suzy'. In her own room, looking out on the bay, I imagine that Suzy had as many hours of desolation, as all the St Mary Peter's lowest form put together, but she was inscrutable and there was always the end of the week. There used to be a lit-up look on her face at the sight of the bus and it can not have been all that different from the country bus we were used to in Malaya, except for the cold. There were the same women on their way into market — the same chickens or ducks with legs bound together — the same stops at the farms, to unload orders from town, the same chattering of local gossip. After a while, Suzy carved out her own place in Argyll and they all liked her, but still there was the 'baby doll' attitude. She did not object that they talked to her slowly and carefully, as if she had not better English than any one of them. They would watch her greet me and then enquire about her health and how she was getting on at the 'Hoose in the Bay' and had she taken to the fishin' yet. Perhaps they might tell her it was time she showed Mistress Janet how to try her hand at the famous Chinese cooking . . . and ask her about some of the dishes they had heard of in the new Chinese Restaurant in Oban that had been opened for the tourists.

Then Suzy and I would go walking down the brae and Suzy snuggling into the warm duffle coat, she had had for

Christmas. Her feet must be getting used to the fur-lined leather knee-length boots and her body to the double strength underwear, 'as worn by the men, who had climbed Everest'. Janet had knitted her a scarf, that fitted her, much the way Slievenailra's son's scarf had fitted her that first day. Her gloves were knitted wool mits and her own self was warm with joy for me, that I was with her again and we would tramp the mountains and along the high tide marks on the sands, that stretched to eternity, north or south.

Suzy would assure me that she was not lonely. We walked the brown bracken or the silver sands or the small grassy sheep tracks and we talked and talked and talked, often in Mandarin Chinese, with Malayan thrown in and sometimes English in 'good braid Scots'. She would tell me all that had happened and about the cases in the practice and about how Dr McLean said she was his practice nurse now. He had taught her how to repack the accident bag, so that she could do it in locum tenens, while I was away. Once, he had let her stitch a cut arm — had shown her what must be done and 'how all must be boiled'. He had taken her out on rounds and showed her how to make people well again. The Scots could be ill with fevers, just as every man was, but the Tuan carried magic in his black case. One day a child might be very sick and like to die, and he would give it a small bottle of tablets. In two . . . three days, it would be running about again, when it might have been with its ancestors in paradise. If the Tuan doctor wanted to go fishing, there were days, when she was suppose to 'mind the practice', but he had told her this was a terrible sin for him, only the fish were rising out in the bay and she had only to ring the ship's brass bell that hung on the back wall of the house and he'd come ashore at once, only more quickly . . . There was a plaited rope that pulled the tongue of the bell and it called him.

I would tell her all that went on in school and she was very impressed by it. I think she had the strange aptitude of picking up all I told her by just opening her ears to me. She learnt about history and geography . . . at least as much as I did. She liked me to lend her the lesson books I brought back to Glenmore. We read together. Together we progressed from grade to grade. The winter was gone and the spring came late, that first year, but always it was the same. We knew to look out for the sprigging of the young lambs on the mountains . . . to seek out the blue-bell pools in the hollows, and the shy clumps of primrose and then the cowslips. We found the small orchids, that could never match the orchids of Malaya, but always turned our minds back across the world, to the heat and the colour and the great out-pouring of the splendours of nature. Here there were the rowan berries and the heather . . . ah! the heather and the joy it was to fish the lochs — the pleasure there was in messing about in a small boat and the freedom we had in the holidays, when the whole countryside was ours.

Through that first spring and summer, Mistress Suzy and I came to love Scotland and that love was to last for ever. Both of us inherited a new dimension of thinking, but as always, she kept Malaya warm in our hearts. It might have turned into a dream place, that never existed, if either of us had been alone, but always we talked of it and longed for it and in the evenings, Grandfather encouraged us to talk about it and tell him all the small details. In exchange, he told us stories of Scotland and adventures from the war years . . . great tales of Glenmore, that matched the romance of Bonnie Prince Charlie, at least to our way of thinking.

Then the year was up and we were to go home for the holidays and again we flew the world, but we were wiser this time. Mistress Suzy wore her starched white jacket and the black cotton trousers, the wide round straw hat, ready for disembarkation and I had packed my summer clothes for Christmas. In a way, I could hardly believe that Kuala Lumpur had ever been real, yet here it was, just the same as ever. Here was Mother of the white shining hair and Father, hugging me against his hard chest. Here were the bright flowers of the sarongs and the saris and the cheongsams . . . the rickshaws, the smart cars, with their colours almost hurting the eyes in the heat and glare, the police in immaculate uniforms and polished boots — the young men on modern motor bikes, who raced along the streets making as much noise as they could, the pavements as crowded as the Tower of Babel might be crowded. . . the perpendicular signs of the Chinese shops, the sweat . . . tongues of every nation . . . prosperous, happy, happy, so very happy, with the colour of the whole world, yet a small part of me was lonely for the shadows of the clouds on a windy day as they chased the Scots mountains to glory.

We had a car . . . a Range Rover in white and it was very smart indeed. The bungalow was smaller than I remembered it, but it was home. It was magic. It was paradise. I had forgotten the luxury of it. The air conditioning, the refrigeration, the long iced drinks. There were so many friends to visit, so many parties to attend, so many to give, and the gentle people that waited on us anticipated every need. Then Christmas was over and gone and all too soon, we must be on our way. This time, I knew no joy of departure. I knew the rigours of school and the loneliness. The tears lay just behind my eyes, but I must not cry. Mother held me too tightly and Father gave me a great amount of pocket money at the last moment and almost undid my calm. I must not weep. I must not lose face. Suzy kept her head lowered and her hands meekly clasped at her waist. I knew she had no mother or father. I knew that she loved my parents and they loved her. I knew that she was suffering the same agonies, that we all suffered that day, but she turned to me, just before we went taxiing along the runway.

"Soon the Tuan, your grandfather will be standing in the hall of the airport, pretending to look at the statue of the great poet, but first, he will have spied out through the window, to see Missie alight the stairs of the plane and Mistress Suzy Chan with her but her warm coat this time. His heart will be filled with a great joy, that the two ladies, who changed the dressings in his accident case will be back to help with the practice and he can go fishing in the bay, if the fish are rising. An old man will not be lonely any more. This is because you are you and I am I, and a great honour has been done to my family, who were all wiped out at one stroke, because a war went sweeping across my country and left nothing but widows and orphans — hungry and with no person to stretch out a hand to them except the Tuan, your father, who has given his life to the British Raj, as it lay dying . . . your mother also to one small Chinese female infant, who was less than the dirt in the gutter . . . who can never forget the debt, she owed your family, did she work for them for a million years, for now she has Father and Mother and Sister . . . she has honourable Grandfather, who counts her a fine Chinese lady, which she was, but is no more, only dust to the feet . . . only for the love between your family and mine . . . and me, I would die with honour for your family, if they asked it of me. I would give away the most precious thing I owned . . . One day, perhaps I will pay my debt, but just for now, know that I know the debt is there, that I owe to your honourable family and I hope the hour will come, when I can repay it . . . "

I did not know what she was thinking about — only that I must hold fast to the thought of Scotland and that they were waiting for me there . . . Grandfather and Janet. God help me!

Grandfather was there, of course, looking at the statue of Robbie Burns, as if he had not been watching us come down the gangway. He was very casual about it all and he told us he had been lonely after us and Slievenailra's son had just been through and a scarf on him that would stretch from here to the Mountain of the Eagles and back again and that he was very depressed, that there was no chance of him being at home for years and years, for he had been picked out for Cambridge University, which was a Sassenach place, miles away. Unfortunately, he was doing well at Gordonstoun and he had passed some exam or another and he had got into Cambridge, which was the best of the universities so there was no going to the islands for a long time and that his mother had her eye on the Diplomatic Service for him and that would be the end. Likely he would finish it off a punt on the Granta and it would be a 'maircy'.

"He was asking after you," Grandfather told Mistress Suzy. "He was surprised that you'd not got your death of cold, but I told him that his coat and scarf had saved your life. He was very gratified."

So here I swung with Mistress Suzy Chan, between one world and the other and each world a different place, and both worlds dear to us — and the years went on, slow first and then faster and faster, with each one merging into the next, yet completely different and still in each world, between us, we kept the other world alive.

2

Grant

THE years had passed. I was twelve, thirteen, fourteen, fifteen, sixteen. I had been a prefect for twelve months. Next term, I was to be head girl. I had responsibility. It was I now, who took the new girls aside and told them that it was not the done thing to cheat. Of course, times had changed but St Mary Peter's had tradition to uphold. During meals, the duty was to watch everybody else and see that their needs were fulfilled, their glasses not empty of water, nor their plates of food. I was to think of that, many years later and smile wryly to myself, when I scrabbled with my bare hands in the earth for the luxury of a potato to eat raw.

For the present, I was content enough. There was one more year at school. Then I was for Edinburgh University to read medicine. My exam levels were good and

I could even start a little way up the ladder in Edinburgh. My standards were excellent, the Reverend Mother told me, but neither of us realised that standards that had high importance at St Mary Peter's might mean little enough, if a world were to be turned upside down and all law come to an end. Survival is what counts . . . a handful of rice . . . a cup of water . . . a hole in a ditch to hide.

I was to be seventeen on Sunday. I was wearing a hunting Stuart kilt and dark green sweater — a duffle coat with wood toggles. The coat had a grand hood, with a lining in the tartan to match and I had only to pull it over my head to shut out the elements. Suzy and I were not going home to Kuala Lumpur this Christmas and I knew that Mother and Father would miss us. Yet Grandfather would be lonely after us here if we went. I was torn between two worlds, but it was to be Hogmanay for Scotland that year and Easter for the Peninsula and the bright streets of Kuala Lumpur. There was plenty to do in Glenmore. I had fished the burn all the morning and if I had a mind to, I could take a gun and go up the mountain after game, but I had bagged enough for the larder for one day and I did not like killing. All I wanted to do was to lean against the sea wall and not even bother to think. It was so very peaceful. I looked up the road and it was as quiet as the Sabbath. Mrs Gregor's hens seemed bored with the day and had come down to the high-tide mark to scrabble round for the bounty of the sea. It was a tranquil place, but soon I must be on my way. There was all next term with the responsibility as head-girl and then there were the crowds of Edinburgh to face and myself gone from a big fish in a small pond to a very small fish indeed, even if I were going straight into Anatomy in the University. I was to be a new girl all over again and I was afraid of the horrors of the dissecting room. I did not even like the sound of the word 'Bodies' but Grandfather had told me that although 'medicine' needed the courage of a pride of lions, they broke you into it gradually.

There was peace in Glenmore and here I might have wished to stay for ever but my peace was shattered, gradually at first and then with a roar of engines that rose to a crescendo. There was a speed-boat, on its way in from the Isles. It was like a bird, the way it took the water. The proud prow lifted high and the wash spreading out aft, setting all the small ships to bow down to it. It was silver and blue and I thought it the most marvellous craft I had ever seen, I, who had seen sampans and junks and liners and yachts, even down to the model galleon in the waiting room of the Prime Minister of Malaya. I recalled the galleon clearly as I watched the silver and blue bird fly in an arc across Glenmore Bay, and come in towards the landing stage at the jetty, not two hundred yards from where I still leaned against the sea wall.

It seemed inevitable that it was going to crash. Then the engine cut and the craft spun on a sixpence and came drifting, drifting in to align itself just so, opposite the bollards . . . There was but one man aboard, and he cast a rope aft and I recognised an expert seaman, from the way he came ashore. He stretched himself, when he had fixed the moorings and came walking along towards where

I still leaned against the lichened wall. He was wearing canvas slacks and a fisherman's sweater in double-knit navy. There was a parcel under his arm. I did not recognise him. He was tall and with fair hair and he wore rope-soled deck shoes. There was a small slope to where I awaited him and he glanced at the lobster creels and the glass floats and the upturned dinghy. Then he stopped opposite where I still waited and I thought it might be better form, if I got to my feet. I knew him from way back. I could not place him, but I knew him. It was a long time ago.

"Hello there! I'd be grateful if you could tell me where Dr McLean lives."

I knew him then and after all, he had not changed much, only just shot up to be a man, not a school-boy any longer, home-sick for the Isles. I remembered the long scarf. Had I not helped Janet to pack it with his warm wool coat, and the Dundee cake, to send after him to Gordonstoun? His hair had been very fair, but it was a shade darker with the years. My head came to the level of his shoulder now, but that other day, we had been of a size. He must have come north from Slievenailra Castle and of course, it was vacation in Cambridge University and he had not thrown himself into the Granta. I remembered the threat of what might happen if he was forced by 'the lady, his mother', into the Diplomatic Service.

"It's not far," I told him, "If you turn round, it's yonder, the four square house with the brass plate. If you wish, I'll take you there, for I'm his grand-daughter. I live there and I've met you before."

I put the hood back off my head and I was glad I had put the black velvet ribbon at the nape of my neck, though why that mattered I could in no way understand. He took one look at me and smiled and said that, of course, he remembered me.

"Who could forget that silver hair?"

He put out a hand to take mine and said 'Virginia' and of course, I'd known that his name was Gareth Grant and he held my hand still and walked along to the granite house . . .

"Gareth!" Grandfather cried and flung the door wide and for the rest of the day, time flew like the silver and blue boat. Slievenailra's son brought the house to life. He brought the glen to life. He set a glow in Suzy Chan's eyes and he made Janet laugh. My Grandfather was back in the old days, when he and Slievenailra had been up in Edinburgh. We talked about every subject under the sun. He was up at Cambridge and he was expecting to go on an expedition to Malaya in a year. He was full of it and he asked me about Kuala Lumpur and about rice cultivation and about the economy and why the Chinese were so much more given to business and the Malayans to the land. He took Suzy Chan and me round the bay in the speed-boat, wrapped her in his coat again. He thrilled us with the speed and with the risks he took, for he could miss a rocky land-face by half a foot and turn off to safety, where there was no time to escape death.

He was casual and friendly. He might have lived in Glenmore all his life. In the main street, he stopped to talk to the ladies, come down to the Village Stores to do some bogus shopping, just to meet him. They were inclined to curtsey to him and explained this to me later.

"He's Slievenailra's only son. He's like to be one of the Lords of the Isles, when his father's deid. Dinna the Doctor's ain bairn ken that he's Scots royalty?"

He asked after their children and their men and he might have been a top politician on his rounds before an election.

He had come specially to deliver a present from his father to Grandfather and if it had been the biggest diamond in the world, it couldn't have brought more pleasure. I knew that Grandfather was a Conan Doyle fan. He had a special locked book case in the surgery with first editions of Conan Doyle. I could never work up such enthusiasm about them as he did, but he read them and re-read them. Now there he was unwrapping two big square volumes and they were in such good condition that they might have been printed yesterday.

"First editions of the Adventures and the Memoirs!" he cried, as if he were talking about God. "The ones published by the Strand. Did you know, Virginia, that the stories appeared in the Strand Magazine first of all and Sherlock Holmes grew to be a living breathing man. He became a cult. People even come to blows as to whether he went to Oxford or Cambridge . . . a man, who never lived at all. He wanted to write historical books, like the White Company and Sir Nigel and in that his mother encouraged him, but it was Sherlock Holmes the public wanted . . . and Sherlock Holmes came to life and he's still alive . . . all over our civilised world. There's fame for you. People go to see his house in Baker Street." He opened first one book and then the other.

"I just have no words I can say. 'Not even foxed and the spines not rubbed.' Where did your father get these magnificent volumes? He might give me the Castle of Slievenailra and not give me such wealth. Believe me, laddie."

Gareth was as young as I, or just nine years short of it. He could not understand nostalgia for the past. He and I had no past worth mentioning. We had not known what it was to grow old and remember.

"Actually it was I, who picked them up in a shop near Charing Cross . . ."

Throughout the whole evening, Grandfather kept going to the cupboard and taking out first one book and then another. He might handle a new-born babe with such gentleness.

"In Charing Cross, he says . . . and no pride of accomplishment of what he found. They don't make books like this any more, Laddie. Don't you understand the sybaritic pleasure it is to read a book you know by heart and hold a first edition in your hand. Look at the gilt on the cover, as bright as the day it left the press."

I could not remember having had such a successful visitor in Glenmore House. Come to that, I could not ever remember a person that made such impression in Malaya visiting the bungalow. He had 'charisma' and that was a word I had just learnt. Now I knew what it meant.

I saw him off from the jetty the next day and he paused just before he went and asked me for my address at home.

"I hope to be in Malaya next year, with the Cambridge project. I'll look your people up and give them your felicitations."

He glanced up at me with the long peak of his cap tilted over his eyes and again I thought of Scarba on a sunny day and how the sea is deep and green. His lashes were dark against the fair hair and they swept the planes of his cheeks.

"Maybe we'll meet in Malaya," he said and I shook my head and told him it was long odds. "We come and we go, Suzy Chan and I."

"I'll call and see your people anyhow — tell them how happy you are and that you've got an expert knowledge on how to whip the loch for trout — good shot with a twelve-bore too. You could live in a land where another might die. You're a lassie for all seasons."

It was a great joke for him, but I was sad to see him go, for the life of the glen went with him.

"Slievenailra's on Turnish but you know that. It's south a good way, till you're clear of Skye. Then you come to the Sound of Turnish and veer west — tide must be right. The water runs every way and there's a churning on the surface and a grinding to the hull as if all the demons of the deep were going to take the boat to the sea bed. It's easy if you watch it. Don't worry."

He started the engine and began to edge out from the shore.

"Haste ye back," I called and he turned his head at that.

"We'll meet again, you and I," he said. "The world's a small place. I will see thee at Philippi."

Then there was a great roar of the engines and he was gone like an arrow across the water and I knew that it was one chance in a thousand that I would ever see him again. Tomorrow was Sunday and I would be seventeen. I had a year to fill in at school and today it did not seem all that important to be Head-girl of Saint Mary Peter's. Then I had six-seven years, and it was a long time, to work in Edinburgh. Then home to Malaya perhaps or back to Glenmore and there were a great many people to meet, but never one like the son of Slievenailra. He had not turned his head again, as he went fast to the south. He might remember Glenmore as a happy day, but no more than that. He was not dreading the Diplomatic Service any more. His career lay one way and mine lay another. He had no way of knowing that I had fallen in love with him, yet I was wise enough to know it as infatuation. For a while, he might inhabit my dreams between waking and sleeping, as a knight in white armour. There was no time for love in my life. I was programmed for a career and that was that, was that. Yet I had waved to the wake of his speed bird and I had whispered into the wind.

"Haste ye back."

★ ★ ★

'Turn around! Turn around!' the song goes and life speeds on its way. That was how it was. I was at the jetty and the boat was out of sight and I might have just turned around and a full year had gone. It was not possible that time could match the silver bird.

Easter was past and Suzy and I had been to Malaya and school term had started and over and another term started and done and Christmas was upon us. I had not heard from Slievenailra's son and I hardly believed that he had ever come to call at Glenmore.

The subject that held attraction was my birthday — that and the fact that school was finished for ever. My eighteenth birthday was here and we were all sitting in the house and Janet had produced a splendid cake with a great many candles. Outside, the night was rough, but within, it was safe and snug. The rollers might be breaking against the garden wall and the men would stand all night in the well of small ships. The sea might have the appearance of being able to overpower the land — mountain and town and city, till water covered the face of the earth again, but I knew that my world was impregnable. Far off in the Peninsula, my people would be remembering that it was my birthday. I thought of the air-conditioned bungalow and ice drinks, cold in glasses, the slippered feet of the Indian manservant against the polished floor . . . the cane furniture. Malaya was my exotic land, safe against time. Easter was a happy memory and again soon, we were due on a visit. I had had my birthday present and a letter too and the letter told me all about the new Range Rover, Mother wanted to have a white car again, but Father had held out for a gold colour. It would not show the dust. They had sent me a wrist watch, a product of Switzerland. It had done the round trip from Switzerland to Malaya and back again to Scotland.

"It is nothing. We do it all the time," said Suzy Chan and she was wearing the black cotton trousers and the starched shirt, with the high collar and the slits at the side and she was the old Suzy again.

Then Grandfather had an important announcement to make, for soon I would be away to Edinburgh. That might leave Suzy lonely and he had consulted with Janet. Suzy was to become a trained nurse. It was all arranged, for her heart was in healing, just like the priests in the Snake Temple in Penang, that we were always blethering about. Suzy had learned more from 'yon expensive school' than ever I had. More than that, she had taken tuition from the Minister in the evenings, when he had finished his work in the parish. There were things they called exams, but Suzy was as clever as a cart-load of monkeys. He, himself, had a bit of influence in Edinburgh Infirmary. The 'head witch doctor' there and he were old friends. More than that there was the question of the fishing in the Bay. I could not believe what he was saying. It added up the fact that while I attended the University, Suzy was to train as a nurse. When we were through, we might come home and run Glenmore National Health Service without him. He was considering spending the last years of his life out in the Bay after the fish, or up the hill with his gun. It all went on for a long time, so that Suzy could accept privilege without loss of face and she'd make a finer nurse, than many a lassie, for had she not had her initial training in Glenmore under himself?

I shall never forget the look on Suzy's face. She was unreadable, but then she always was, only that now she was lit up from within. Her eyes shone with gladness and her hands gripped together in her lap, knuckles white. Janet went to kiss her and so did I, but there was little emotion about her. She just sat there looking at the clasped hands, her voice very low. She seemed to have left Glenmore and to be in a limbo of her own.

"How can I say thank you? To your family, I owe all that I am. Now again, more honour is poured out to me — more happiness than I can bear. I was a small child, when your mother, with the moon in her hair, stopped the jeep and lifted me from the roadside, from the body of my dead mother. I had been lying against her all night and in the morning, the sun came and still she did not breathe and she was cold. I knew then there was nothing any more, but to die. Your mother came with the winged hat on her head and she picked me up. She took off her black jacket and there was gold on the sleeves of it. She did not care that I was dirty. She protected me warm in it and she tucked me into a rush basket. She put me beside her in the truck and away to a great ship. After a while she found a place for me with a good Chinese family, but she promised that she would come back for me, when the fighting was over and she came back. She told me never to weep for my mother, my mother had gone to paradise, with my father — together."

It was the first time she had ever told me the whole story, though perhaps my grandfather had heard about it. It would not be good form to speak any more now. I knew her well by this and I knew that only great emotion had made her talk out. I would get it from her another day, but just for now, it was best to keep silent and resume the birthday party. The phone rang, as always it rang at awkward moments. I had no way of knowing that another part of my life was slotting into the pattern. My grandfather went to answer it, and I thought how Suzy had been told not to weep for her mother, that her mother had gone to paradise with her father. I had no inkling of the news that was on its way to me and how truth was always stranger than fiction. Grandfather came back into the room after fifteen minutes and no word out of him to say if he had a visit to do up the brae. He just sat there in silence. Then after a time, he got up and poured himself a dram and gulped it down . . . went back to his chair by the fire. Soon, he was up and pouring another dram to bring it over to me, bade me drink it at one gulp. I thought maybe he meant it for my birthday toast.

The Glenlivet lipped the top of the glass and I looked at him in surprise. "Drink all of it?"

It was what they said at Communion. 'Drink ye all of it.' It filled me with fire. It burnt my throat and my gullet and set me aflame and so that I gasped and drew in a great breath.

"Yon was news from abroad, but the line was bad. Jeanie, at the post, had an awfu' time to cope with it, but she did fine. It was hard to hear what he was saying."

We sat and wondered what was wrong, for his head was in his hands now.

"My puir wee lassie and her hair as white as yours is and the loveliness that lived in her face and her gentle soul . . ."

Fear had come into the room.

"Is it bad news?" Janet asked him and

he kept his head in his hands and said "Aye."

Then after a while, he pulled himself together and looked at me, caught my eyes with his and held them.

"You'll have to be very brave, Lassie. There's something I have to tell you and no escape for either of us from the telling. I had it from Malaya not ten minutes since. Hold yourself ready, and remember that I'm wi' ye and Suzy Chan and Janet — and Glenmore — Suzy Chan was in the same awful grief and she but a wee bairn. You'll not find yourself left on the side of the road, not like she was, till your mother found her and wrapped her in the Wren jacket and laid her in a rush basket."

"Is Mother dead?" I asked him and my mouth was too dry for words. The phrase went over and over in my head. The words Suzy had said not so long ago. "My mother had gone to paradise with my father . . . "

Grandfather had told me, or was it some nightmare that Suzy had been in the same awful grief? That meant that my father was dead as well as my mother.

His puir wee lassie and her hair as white as mine . . . and the lovely face and the gentle ways.

It could not be real. It was as false as if I watched all that was happening, a celluloid transparency, thrown on a silver screen. The cake was there and the lingering smell of eighteen wax candles, blown out. I could not remember blowing them out nor recall any wish . . . only remember the harsh shrill of the telephone. I had not cut the cake. The icing was still intact with its 'HAPPY BIRTHDAY, VIRGINIA' and the cake knife waited for my hand but the phone had interrupted the ceremony, or had it been Suzy Chan and her revelation about her tragedy . . . It had happened to me now the same tragedy or had it? It was not possible. The china cups gleamed and the peat glowed and butter ran down the sides of the scones and I remembered the taste of it in my mouth, yet my mouth was tasteless. The gold watch, that had travelled all the way from Switzerland to Kuala Lumpur and then back again to me in Scotland, it was on my wrist. The velvet-lined box was on the table.

My mind flew off at a tangent. Almost certainly, the watch would have been sent direct from Switzerland to me, by special order. I had not examined the postal package, only torn it open and thrown the paper in the basket. I stood up now as stiffly as an old woman and went to retrieve the wrapping. It was post-marked 'Kuala Lumpur' and the writing was Mother's and it seemed very important with all those foreign stamps, yet I knew there perhaps was no importance in it. I folded the brown paper carefully and put it down on the table with the string tied up in a small hank and I had undone the knots and left the string neatly, and thought that it was the last message I would ever have from them. But there had been the letter — white car or gold?

The room was silent, except for the storm in the chimney and the whip of the sleety rain against the window glass. The slow knell of the clock in the hall was too like a passing bell.

"Mother?" somebody said, "Not Father too? Not both of them?"

"Both of them," Grandfather said and

I had a flash back to myself at my prayers and he by my bed all the long years ago. It had been safe and loving and an anodyne for home loneliness.

"God bless Mother and Father and keep them safe . . . "

God had not kept them safe, but it was not true. It had never happened. It was not happening now. It was a Chinese puppet shadow show, and no end to it.

"It was a road accident. They were killed instantly. That was Slievenailra's son on the phone . . . the laddie, Gareth Grant. He's in Malaya on some project from Cambridge. He said they died with honour, same way they lived. It was hard to make out what he was telling me. He's in Kuala Lumpur now, and he'll act for us. We're to stay here together and wait. He'll send all details and he'll see to what has to be done. He said we're not to be breaking our hearts, for they were together and happy. It's what they'd have wanted. He said I was to look after you, Virginia, and one day, he'll see you again . . . and tell you."

"The line went dead on us and that was all I got, but he does not want us to fly out there. No time, he said . . . not in the tropics. He'll do what must be done and I've got faith in his father's son. He's the man I'd pick for such a task, but God have mercy on us all! You're so like my girl, that it's breaking my heart to look at you and I love you as much as ever I loved my ain lassie . . . but you are my ainly lassie now."

Suzy Chan's face was a mask of tragedy. I had never seen her weep, but now slow tears ran down her perfect face and her hand was in mine, a Dresden hand.

"She was a good woman. Good was the weaving of her life. You are like her, Virginia. You're a strong one. You must mourn your honourable parents. Then you will cast off sorrow. You *must* cast it off. You are going to love life just as she did in her turn — looking for the poor ones and the sick ones — and now and again, picking up a lost soul and wrapping it against the things that are happening in the world. We can't do without people like those, just gone to God, but we know that their souls are happy in paradise with their ancestors.

Yet I cry, I, who never cry in all my life, because they were my family too, the only family I remember in truth . . . and soon, we put away sorrow. One day, you and I, we set out to hold back the tide, little missie. This I know, though I do not know how or where or when, only that it will come about . . . "

She was usually so silent that I looked at her in surprise, yet she was far wiser than I. She was more cheerful and helpful in that sad house than I. I only wanted selfishly to get out of it and away — back to the tropical peninsula, where I might find it all as it had been, with the crowded streets of Kuala Lumpur, where there was life all about, with people teeming the streets, and the youth and vivacity and all the nations gathered together, where the shops were bright and where the cars flashed by, where dark faces smiled, where a buffalo, against all rules, might come strolling along the street and snarl up all the traffic and look so unperturbed about his breaking of the law . . . where people might still laugh and be happy and live. I thought of all the small things and perhaps I forgot the discomforts. Maybe I forgot the serpent in the Garden of Eden, but now I had been locked out of it for ever. I wanted to come zooming down out of the sky or maybe along the lines to the splendid railway station, that was still the pride of Kuala Lumpur. I wanted home. How much I wanted home, yet here was home too! I waited in the stone house in the bay and the news came slowly, for my bright land was far away. Gradually it arrived — by cable, by telex, by British Diplomatic bag, in cuttings from newspapers, the Straits Mail, the Malay Mail, in solicitors' letters, in documents tied with red tape.

There was a description of the funeral in the Malay Times. The Memorial Service was any day of giving thanks to God, for the loved ones he had gathered to Himself.

The obituary notice in a late Times and Telegraph, was British Raj, which still smouldered out there. My mother had served with honour in the WRNS. Father had been a Commander in the Royal Navy. They had a large circle of friends in Malaya and were well known for their kindness, their cheerfulness and their love for mankind. Here was the type of people, who were irreplaceable . . .

Then the Straits Mail again . . . 'It was a comfort to know that Commander and Mrs John Stuart are laid to rest beside John and Constance Stuart, near the bungalow, which had replaced the residence where old John Stuart and his wife slept.'

I watched the bay for Gareth Grant. That was all the sense I had. I ignored the delays of the law. I ignored the long miles that stretched between my two worlds. Sometimes, Grandfather phoned Gareth in Kuala Lumpur but the telephone was a thing of irritation, with the crackling of atmospherics.

Well I knew that no silver bird would fly across the Bay, yet every day I watched for it. Always the post arrived carried up the brae by the old postie and if he had a special 'foreign' letter for us, he called out to us from a hundred yards away. So we got the letters of condolence and the newspaper clippings and the solicitors' communications and at last a personal letter to me from Gareth himself. It was signed 'GRANT' in that imperial way he had. Grandfather was out on a case and Suzy was with him. Janet, was away to the Home Stores to do the messages. I took the letter up to my room and wondered why my heart was beating as fast as if I had run all the way to the jetty to meet the silver bird.

It was on the thin stuff of Air Mail and it was postmarked Kuala Lumpur, the writing misted for a moment, then I read his letter . . .

'Dear Virginia. I have had the news from Glenmore and as I sit here writing this, I picture you as you were that day, on the sea wall, when I came up the cobbled slip from the boat . . . the tartan kilt and the duffle coat with the wood toggles and the surprise when you put back the hood of the coat and I saw the young silvered hair.

'I must say at once, there is no gratitude due to me for anything I have done here. It has been my honour to help in any way I could. I was on the spot. It was easily done. Your name is powerful in Malaya and so many people were pleased to help.

'I have told the full story to your Grandfather. Now I send the details to you and you will show the letter to Suzy Chan.

'That tragic day, your mother and father had collected the new Rover. Maybe they were still arguing about the colour, but it all happened so easily and it was such an unnecessary petty thing. You know the track that leads in from the metalled road to the house and the little kampongs along the way . . . the reed roofs and the open verandas.

'You know the fuss there is if the Chinese chef lets a pig stray near the Malayan quarters and what a joke your mother made of it! They say Chinese do not cry, but Sam Wong wept by the grave. It was Sam's child, Lily who ran out under the car. Lily saw the pig had escaped from its bamboo enclosure pen, she went flying out across the track, aged two and head-high to a grass-hopper. One moment, she was playing on the veranda and the next she was under the front wheels of the car. I imagine that your mother may just have had time to see the black cotton trousers and

91

white T-shirt and recognise Lily Wong. It's a strange thing that Lily was the great grand-daughter of the old Chinese, who was chef to John Stuart the first, and who saw the Japanese shoot him. Maybe your mother forgot the great tree, she herself called The Tree of Heaven. She turned the wheel and by doing that, she saved Lily Wong, but the car took the tree at speed. Put it to yourself that they went straight from happiness into happiness together, unmarked and unblemished and so very honourably. Perhaps they had done all the tasks life had set for them. I don't know. I only know what people have said to me here and it seems to me that I know your people, have known them . . .

'It was easy enough to get the bungalow packed up and the stuff sent off by sea but it was with sadness I did it . . . picked what I thought you might like, but memory is the important commodity. Hold it close! Hold it close that *they* are together and happy. They will know you have the ability to seek out your chosen path, though perhaps there's a change in that. I am more than pleased that you have given up the idea of Edinburgh for the next few months and that you and Suzy will stay in Glenmore for your grandfather's sake just for a while. It fits in. God! How it fits in!

'We'll meet again, you and I. I made up my mind about that the day you waved me goodbye and "Haste Ye Back". The 'Haste Ye Back' sent out a hand that has held me fast.

'Just for now, I'm enclosing in this letter, the strangest thing I found in the bungalow, another letter with an enclosure . . . the most precious thing to my mind at least. You will know the history of it, but you may never have seen it. Now it belongs to you.

'Your grandfather Stuart had had this letter from your father, telling him about the WRNS officer, he was to wed. In it, were enclosed these two locks of hair. The old man put the letter in the safe . . . fire-proof, it was and he trusted to its keeping a safe secret. It must have been the last thing he did, before he set the torch to the petrol soaked house.

'I imagine the last thing he remembered was this envelope and the glad news it had brought them . . . that life would go on.'

I curled the lock of white hair round my finger, went to the glass and held it against my cheek and it was no different from my own hair. Perhaps there is as little difference between life and death and one must believe one must 'cling heaven by the hems'.

'Keep this letter safe, Virginia. It might be a good thing to have something to hold on to, if the going gets tough . . . a talisman . . .'

I showed the letter to Suzy, when she came in and she touched the locks of hair with her lips, made that small gracious bow she often did, hands joined together in front of her, as if she prayed. Then she smiled at me and tried to lift my spirits.

"Maybe the going gets tough for both of us. I think maybe healing in a great city is not like the healing in this small mountain village. Perhaps in the river Forth, the fish do not rise so excellently, so that a man has no time to be sick, but must hurry for his nets and his boat . . ."

She smiled at me and the sun came out across the room and that is how I will always see her, trying her best to heal my sad soul.

Then she turned the letter from Gareth over to put it back in its envelope and saw the small scribbled post-script, which I had missed. It was on the last page and I had not seen it but I saw it now and little I realised what an important thing it was. Perhaps it changed the rest of my life. Perhaps it made no difference whatever. Gareth had written an after-thought. I read it now and was no wiser, only for the thought that it was like the message that the lawyer's clerk, Wemmick, had left for Pip, in Great Expectations.

'Don't go home' Wemmick had written, but now Gareth had a different message for me and I understood it not at all. 'P.S. Do not go to Edinburgh. Await my arrival in Scotland . . . ' and the same proud signature below that I had come to know, sprawled across the bottom of the last page of all . . .

GRANT

95

3

The Royal College

I SHOWED the letter to Grandfather and asked him about the postscript, but he pretended to know nothing about it and I knew that he was prevaricating. Something had happened, that had not been expected. Perhaps I had been left with very little means. They were young, my parents, and these were difficult times for saving. Against that, I was eligible for State grants for Edinburgh, because of my credits in exams. I did not care one way or another. I was in a darkness of spirit, where there did not seem to be much point about anything. Yet, the sinister quality of the letter attracted my interest and Grandfather lost patience with me.

"Can you no' stop havering about what the laddie meant? He's in charge of your parents' estate . . . took the position out of the kindness of his heart. Small

96

gratitude you show to him. Do you doubt a word he says now?"

He knew all about it and I did not. I was quite sure of it. There had been communications between them and I had been closed out, closed out gently, but closed out all the same. There was some blue-print in the planning of something, which might come about, or which might fail and the wise thing had been to tell me nothing about it. Still, I noticed that the talk about Edinburgh University had dwindled and died and there were no more bright plans. Anxiety possessed me, but I kept silence too and waited.

So Suzy and I passed away the winter in Glenmore and the small rain rained. The Scots mist claimed the mountains and then the snow made scenic beauty, with no comfort, only before the hearth in the sitting room or by the kitchen stove, where sorrow was slowly becoming bearable.

It was a borrowed day, the day it happened. For a week it had rained. All about us, the mountains had been hidden in mist and every burn overflowing. Then that morning, the sun came out and an early lamb was born on the hill. There was still a cluster of Christmas roses in the shelter of the sea-wall, where Janet set a sheet of glass each year, a few celandines in the patch of earth that we called the front garden. Presently, the grassy rise straight across the road from the house would have primroses and then cowslips, but not for a while yet. Just for today, there was sunshine and the mountains clear again and white clouds in the sky and a first lamb on the hill.

Janet and Suzy were busy with the dinner and Grandfather had a patient in the surgery. It was just an ordinary day, but there was a sparkle of happiness in the house. It was a fine thing to go walking down the glen with the duffle bag slung across my shoulder to do the messages.

I was wearing the Royal Stuart kilt, just because I had got a conviction that mourning was not 'for aye'. It was no fit wear for a lassie bereaved, but I had pulled on a heavy knit black sweater, that had a roll-up collar about my ears. My hair was in a pony tail and I had fastened it in the black velvet ribbon bow, in some sort of a gesture to Mother's memory. People were starting to smile at me again. I had done my duty and stayed by 'my ain folk' and the wee Chinese lassie with me, to comfort him in the loss of his 'lassie'. I had seen that his heart was not broken, as much as my heart was, for 'was not Mistress Alison my mother, and she had run as a child in this same glen . . . and she as like to what I was the day, as, two peas in a pod'.

There was no sudden silence now in the Village Stores as there had been, when I came in. There were few people there and some with Gaelic on their tongue and their voices singing against the bare rafters of the roof. It was a shop, that sold everything.

Mrs Mackintosh was waiting to serve me and remarking on the grand day it was. There was some politeness of talk between us all and interested questions about what was going on in the Doctor's house. So Andy Muir had come to consult Himself? There 'wid be naething between them but talk of the feshing, so there was no haste to me. I might bide my time. Mrs Mackintosh had some pork steaks fresh in from Inverness and she had put some by for me. Janet would only have to lay them in the pan.

I thought of the pig, that had strayed across the road from its bamboo compound and how unclean is a pig to the Malayan. Always my mind went skeetering away on these journeys. My mother had gone to her death. 'Puaka' they called them in Malaya, the earth demons, that could haunt trees. The Malayans would not take rubber from a haunted tree. The Puakas went about the country in bands and they hunted men, but they could not cross water. The people in the Kampongs wore amulets against them . . .

Then I was back in the Home Stores again with the clean cold of the sea blowing in when the door opened and the lilt of the Scots accent in my ears.

"Are you no' away to the University any more? Och, mebbe 'tis best to bide here in the Bay and see after your folk. Isn't it a great pity that if you did get your degree you'd no be in time to tak' ower from Himself? He's spent himself in the war and he finds the hills a torment. It wid tak' ye six-seven years to get your

100

'pairchment' and Himself will be retired afore then. Besides, it mightn't be proper for a lady doctor to take Glenmore. 'Tis work for a man and all that's wrong wi' half the folk is the Scots surfeit of whisky. You'll be aiming for higher places, for foreign countries, where they need doctors like the desert needs watter. You could nae pass your fine career in a wee place like Glenmore where a doctor has no ease but in the shooting and in the feshing . . . and we'll never get anither like the Master above, wi' the humanity he carries in his braist."

A woman came in through the door.

"Did ye ken ye had a visitor, Mistress Stuart?" she asked me and was the centre of interest in the shop at once. She realised that I had no knowledge of the very important thing that had happened. Otherwise, I would not be idling my time.

I was trying to assimilate the fact that Glenmore didn't expect me to take over the practice and that was shock enough without this.

"There was a quiet car went up the road ten minutes past . . . stopped at the

Doctor's hoose . . . no sound out of it. A body would na' ken if 'twere standing still. There was a gentleman at the wheel. He had a look of Slievenailra's laddie, him in the speedy boat a whiles past, and two big hounds, setting up in the back seat, like two gentlemen theirselves and one of them gold and one black. I think maybe there're The Laird's shooting dogs . . . Slievenailra himself."

"I have a fresh batch of bread baked and eggs and butter and cream straight from the cow . . . " said Mistress Mackintosh understanding the worry of an unexpected guest. "Janet can run and fetch it, or mebbe you'd wish I leave it over mysel'?"

They were good neighbours, the people of Glenmore. I had had many kindnesses at their hands. I knew their small physical ailments. With no medical training in the world, I might advise a cold compress or to bathe with hot water. I might have had full training at the Snake Temple in Penang, with the reverence that was shown to me, yet now I knew they did not expect me to inherit the practice of Glenmore. Still I knew, or thought I knew, that Gareth Grant at this moment was in the house and I not there to open the door to him. I made my excuses as gracefully as I might and no hurry only the hurry of my heart. I finished my shopping and took the bread and the cream and the eggs too. I said goodbye, said carelessly that it probably was Slievenailra's son, who always came without warning. Then I walked at a normal speed up the road and sure enough there was a car parked, a car that matched the silver bird. It was just as the woman had described it in the shop — a car, that would make no sound. It was dark maroon and a gold stripe to it and the two dogs sat sedately in the back seat and did not even turn their heads, when I spoke to them, so superior they were, Labradors, one gold and one black, and mighty bored with the waiting . . . and the long drive and the waste of a day, that should have been taken up with retrieving game.

He had been there some time, for Janet had put the pheasants in the oven, Suzy had cut the game chips and was working on the bread sauce. They had not spoken to him. He had been in the surgery with Grandfather and I thought that perhaps they had transacted a deal of business in my absence and now was the time, when I was to be told whatever it was I had to be told. I gave the bag to Janet and she exclaimed with delight over the cream. Suzy maybe knew the state my heart was in, but she concentrated on finishing the chips and began to make the noodle dish that had sliced cucumber in it and maybe grated coconut, and this was a foreign place for such food. I straightened my kilt and put a hand to the black bow on my hair and saw only happiness in their faces.

"You're to go straight in. It's yourself, he's come to see."

They were sitting by the fire with a dram to their hands. He got to his feet and he was just as I remembered him, only the fair hair slightly fairer and his face tanned with the sun. He took my hand in his and his eyes went to the black velvet bow. Then he stood me off and looked at me — the white hair, the black sweater, the Royal Stuart tartan, the skein of worry, I had about what was in the house to offer him and amusement about that. Here I was then, he thought to himself, this colonial orphan, who had come bumbling into his life with no right in the world.

I managed to go through the motions of being the British memsahib, the lady from the Peninsula, born to privilege but with privilege no more. Grandfather tried to put me at my ease, but I hardly listened to him, said something about everything having been arranged satisfactorily but he had a case waiting to see. It was any doctor's excuse.

I stood toe to toe with Slievenailra's son and my head was level with his shoulder and I liked him fine in the moleskin jacket with the shooting patch for the walnut of the stock of his gun, with the dark lashes against the fair hair and with the deep green of Scarba seas in his eyes.

I overcame the awkwardness with a joke about the two dogs in the car and the business of getting them in to sit by the fire, which they did with the most wonderful elegance, one at either side of the hearth. Then I was half taking in what he was trying to tell me. He had spoken to me for quite a while and yet I had not listened to him, not properly.

"Why did you tell me I wasn't to go to Edinburgh?" I asked him point blank at last, quite sure that if I had listened to what he had said, I would have known it.

"I have the credits," I finished and he understood the doubts I had and the fears. He threw a sheaf of bright pamphlets, he had taken from his case down on the table beside my hand.

"There's Malaya for you, described by their Tourist Agency. I've seen it for myself . . . the snags behind the bright lights. I've lived the heat by day and the mosquitoes by night. Here's an emergent nation. You were born there and you lived there, you know it far better than I'll ever know. It wants help and it wants your help."

He went on with it, starting about my people, how young they were to die and how they had had no time to be ready. I was sole legatée and the estate was finalised. There was not all that much money, but I, myself was beyond price.

Here he was awkward and not able to express what he wanted to say.

"It's a country which has lost two people it could ill afford to lose. There's a mixture of nations out there. They want people like you and like Suzy Chan. They want doctors and nurses, as desperately as a man wants the future and maybe you're home-sick for the colour and the sunshine and the smiles?"

It went on for a long time and at last I got the gist of what he was trying to tell me. There was the Company, for which my parents had worked and my grandfather Stuart. The Company had come seeking me, for I was a rare bird, Malayan born with Malaya my tongue and Mandarin Chinese and English and God knew what else. Suzy Chan might be carved in gold for her value to the country, but if she had nursing degrees, she too was beyond price. As a doctor, I was the answer to prayer. Did I realise that there were still witch doctors in Malaya? "They're illegal but they grow like weeds . . . but you know all that. Why am I trying to teach *you*?"

Then he was off on another track.

"There's a place called the Royal College of Surgeons in Dublin, Ireland, but you'll know that too. They liaise with the Company in Malaya. Malaya sends them students and they send back doctors. There are other emergent nations, that are glad to do the same thing. The government cover all expenses and there are no strings attached to it. If you wish to come back here to Glenmore, there will be no objection, but I don't know if you've ever counted the years? Your grandfather will be past climbing the hills and tramping the tracks. There's not time enough left . . . "

Gareth was well aware of the swift sadness of what I now realised. The will lay on the table and he swept it up and put it out of sight into the slimness of his leather case and went on. He had discussed the whole affair with Dr McLean and there were no problems. There were hospitals in Dublin, who would be glad to take Suzy as a probationer nurse. It was only a step across the sea to Ireland and there would be Glenmore to visit.

"It's virtually settled. It wants your

signature on a piece of paper and you can start out on your fine careers, you and Suzy. Did you know that Amah — the word 'amah' is derived from the Portuguese, 'ama', meaning a nurse? It's what she wants, what she's always wanted, but it's just to be near you."

He stood up and watched me in the mirror over the fire.

"You're a very independent lassie. If you insist on Edinburgh, your education will be up to your grandfather and he's happy about this. If you go to Dublin, you work your own passage, I'll have to speak out about this. Don't think you'll owe Malaya anything. Your people paid that country over and over for what it's anxious to do for you now."

It was a moment and the signature was done and all thanks to himself put aside. Then Grandfather was back in the room and Suzy and Janet and all of us solemn, as we toasted the future. Grandfather was holding my chin in his hand and looking in my eyes as if he wanted to read my thoughts, but I did not know them myself, only felt a great sadness, because I had not realised that one day he would be too old to walk the hills.

"Your great-grandfather was a graduate of the Royal College," he told me. "You'll not be breaking any fresh ground yonder in Dublin. When you get to RCSI go in by the side door in York Street and walk along the corridor past the Anatomy Room. You'll see his name in gold paint, though maybe it's fading a wee bit by this. He won some Memorial Prize or another, got gold sovereigns into his hand for it. I daresay they still had trams in the streets then. He spent the coin to take his lassie to the Hospital Dance and that night he asked her to wed him. She was to be my mother and she was a lovely woman, the belle of the ball that night, or so my father always told me, but doesn't it show you what a small place the world is and how fate turns man's plans agley and that's what Robbie Burns said — and that's what I told you the first day I clapt eyes on you . . . "

Gareth had been there that day too, winding his scarf round Suzy to keep her warm. For a moment, I recalled it, as if it was happening all over again. Then it was time for dinner and then Suzy and

I sat on the rug and listened to the plans for what was to come. We built castles in the air and we heard about the fine place that Ireland was.

I would have to be prepared for a shock, I, who was so set on snakes. There was not one snake in the whole country, for hadn't St Patrick banished all of them? I couldn't go trying to find a snake to teach me healing. I would just have to use the ordinary more modern methods. Did I think I might manage to make do with them?

The son of Slievenailra could not stay the night and he said that he was sorry for that. We took the dogs up a track for a walk and then it was time for him to go. He was glad to get away. As he said, this was the end of his stewardship and I thought I had been a burden now taken off his shoulders. It had been a long and boring task and he had probably regretted the impulse, that had made him take it on in the first place.

He opened the back door of the car and the dogs jumped in and sat solemnly, side by side, looking to the front and no doubt, as ready as he was to be on their way home.

The car crept along the road and up the hill and no sound out of it. Grant had his own life to lead. Now he was free of Virginia Stuart and her Estate and the settling up of her career. Likely we would never meet again. How could we? Yet I sighed, as I watched the car disappear and I whispered it into the wind, knowing well that he could not hear it.

"Haste ye back!" I said and I was lonely to see him go.

It was strange the way his visit banished the hopelessness and the sense of loss, that had come darkly on Glenmore. Gareth Grant might have been a magician, with the way he took all our minds and turned them inside out, turned light from darkness and made smiles from tears, caused us to look forward.

Edinburgh might never have existed for Grandfather, with the old memories of Dublin, that possessed him now. There was so much to be done and we had preparations to make, but first of all, would he be all right when we were both away? If we asked it once, we asked him a thousand times and Mistress Janet gave a small sniff every time, for had she not managed the household for all the years since Mistress McLean, his lady, lay dead? It went round and round in a circle of question and answer, but Suzy and I both felt guilty of the worst crime in the soldier's book, for we were deserting him. The house would be empty without us and all our little businesses, without the talk of what went on at school and what went on in the practice. Who was to change the things in the accident bag and Janet assured us dryly that she had done it for forty years or thereabouts. She'd manage.

There had been so much preparation to make in so short a time, but now here was the same familiar Air Port and our luggage gone up the moving slide. Here was I in Grandfather's arms and I thought he might never let me go. Janet had come to see us off and we were in pseudo high spirits, for there was a deep misery to each one of us, that must never be acknowledged. He should have said "Haste ye back", but he changed the formula.

"If ye dinna fancy it yonder, lassie, let ye both get on the plane home and come back to the glen."

We laughed and pretended that we did not care, but we did care and very much indeed. There was a pain to it that was almost not to be borne. There was a relief that I was ashamed of, when the plane had taken off and lonely he looked, down there on the tarmac, staring after us, but we must turn our back on him, no, not that exactly. We must put away what had been, on a shelf and remember it and come back to it again and again . . . In no time at all, we were coming in to the Aer Lingus landing ground and here was another foreign country, a place of small patchwork fields, and such a green as I had never seen. Here was Scotland over again, where people had time to be interested in your business, place like Malaya, where time was not of the first importance but the green of it — the brilliant green! The Customs man was interested in Suzy Chan and myself. He forgot the importance of speeding traffic on its way. Only think of it! Two young ladies on their way to study medicine, and nursing, two young ladies from Malaya. Was it to 'The National' we were going? Ah sure, we'd love Dublin and there'd be no loneliness to either of us, for the people had friendly hearts.

The people had friendly hearts, I thought. How kind a sentence it was and there was no need for us to open all 'our traps'. By that he meant our luggage. Our parents would be lonely after us and when we told him we had no parents, it embarrassed him for a moment, for he would never have mentioned it, for the world, if he had known and would we go on out through Customs and good luck go with both of us!

"There's a quality about Dublin that's kin to the statue of Liberty, that noble statue with the up-held torch, that stands at the entrance to New York Harbour.

'Give me your tired, your poor . . .
Your huddled masses yearning to
    breathe free.
Send these, the tempest tossed to me.
I lift my lamp beside the golden
    door . . . '"

I remembered what Grandfather had said and here was proof of it, that a Customs official should quote poetry to Suzy Chan and myself . . . and in a way, the verse described us, and it seemed that Ireland was lonely with the waiting for us. It was a grand welcome and quite suddenly, I knew that all would be well. Here was no hard foreign country. Here life was going to take a new surge to it. Here I was to know such happiness as maybe I had never known and it was all going to end happily. I knew it at the moment, he chalked all the bags and bade us both welcome to the land of saints and scholars, as if he were the Statue of Liberty himself. Then there was the bus in to the centre of Dublin and it was any city, Dublin, yet not quite. There was a smell of malt about it and coffee — and a casual kindliness, that was starting to make itself felt. If we wanted Leeson Street, it was possible that a taxi might be best but a bus would suit just as well. It wasn't far.

Round a corner now and a swift halt to the taxi and the man was offering to carry up our bags for us. It was a two storied house on a corner opposite a big hospital, with some steps to the hospital door. Two old ladies were twittering with anxiety and then came a steep enclosed staircase and at last, the flat. The flat was a wonder to our eyes and it was to be ours for five or six years. It seemed impossible that Suzy and I could have such freedom, such control of our own lives. The old ladies lived on the ground floor and they were very Cranford-genteel. They had been forced by circumstances to let off the top flat and I shall never forget the glory of that top flat, if I live to be a hundred.

Here was a licence indeed, for all that Suzy had to live as an intern in the hospital a stone's throw away. In five minutes, if she walked fast, she could be in the flat and I was to be a permanent resident there. I had known the luxury of the bungalow in Malaya and I had lived the peace of Glenmore and the hard winters and the good, sensible food, but here was the stuff of teenage freedom.

It was a big flat, for it was out of fashion with the nineteen seventies. It was Georgian and the rooms were graceful and lovely, even if the furniture was well past its best. There were two bedrooms and a drawing room and the kitchenette was the landing at the top of the stairs, but the drawing room was a delight, facing right across to the hospital. The windows had balconies, but the ladies told us they were not safe. For all their danger, they were beautiful in a manner that was gone for aye, with curved tops to the windows and wrought iron railing to the balconies . . . and the gas stove might be vintage but it worked, when we had the coin to put in the meter. There was a coal fire and one could buy a sack from a man, who called every week. The furniture was wonderful, a three piece suite, rather the worse for wear, a table that might be Victorian and which had seen many breakfasts, some upright chairs, near Chippendale — and in the bedrooms, a bed to each room and a washstand with marble top, with dressing tables that jammed their doors, a wardrobe — but the bathroom was magnificent. It had a gas heater and a white bath that was almost big enough to swim in, and it cost very little in the meter and there was a mat made of cork, which would last down eternity.

We were a corner house and just across the street were the little shops, where one could buy anything, butter, eggs, jam, porridge, noodles and curry for Suzy's exotic dishes. The first thing we did was to make a list and go shopping. When we came back we stocked the cupboard and cleaned up the whole place like any industrious housewives. Then we unpacked and claimed the place for our own. We had brought towels and bed linen and china, Janet had seen to that, but I shall never forget the pride I had in this first household of my own and I know Suzy felt it too. They trusted us just as they had trusted us in St Mary Peter's . . . and the flat was so convenient to Suzy's hospital and somebody had seen to it all and in youth, we never gave a thought to whom it might be, the Company presumably, for there were no accounts to be met. For half a second, I identified Gareth Grant with it and then I forgot him, forgot everything except the fact that I was due to register in the Royal College the next day and Suzy was to present herself at the Hospital. Together in the gathering dusk, we sat and looked across the street at the red brick facade . . . wondered what went on there, and did not learn for a very long time that Gareth Grant had arranged the whole set up.

I do not think we slept well that first night. I remember the porridge we had for breakfast next morning and the top of the milk on it in lieu of cream, the boiled eggs, the lovely Dublin bread and the Kerrygold butter and the marmalade, slice after slice.

We were very nervous that morning, but it made no difference to young healthy appetites. We were dressed in our best clothes and had set our courage to face the terror of registering.

Two hours later, I had gone in the York Street door of the Royal College and had walked along the hall, had turned into the corridor and seen my maternal great-grandfather's name in gold paint and he had spent the prize money on the Hospital Dance and had wed my great-grandmother and so had been born my grandfather and then had come Alison

Stuart, nee McLean and that was how I stood there, looking up at the browning board with the gold repainted recently, but hardly in honour only of old Robert McLean.

Then I was in a queue of insignificant nervous young people waiting to register and here was Malaya over again, the Tower of Babel, the sub continental Indians in their white shirts and their straight black hair and deep black eyes, the Africans, with clothes that were too Western for them, and thick lips and kinky hair, the Chinese, solemn faced and earnest and the great proportion of white man, awkward and pink faced, looking too self-conscious and nervous indeed with school tie and Sunday clothes, or maybe more modern sharp gear, faded blue canvas slacks and windcheater . . . and the easy grace to them and always the curly hair and the fine faces, maybe one or two over from England, very proper in their dress, but sophisticated with the accent of the British Raj still in their mouth. I knew it gave them no precedence any more anywhere and perhaps it was a sad bad, thing.

It was all very alphabetical, yet it was not impersonal. The Registrar might look like a hanging judge, but he had a sense of humour and he was very old. He remembered the years. It was an honour to hear that he had known your father or your mother before you . . . had known all about your family before you were born.

"Your mother was a bright girl, Abimbola. It's head of the whole country she is now and good luck to her. When you're writing to her, tell her I recall the night she sang 'Mighty Like a Rose' in the Musical Society the first show we ever had, and brought the show to a halt — never thought she'd end up with white hair, ruling all the medical affairs of Lagos, and great pride to us . . . in her."

I passed with scant notice, for he well knew my tragedy and he had no intention of parading it before the regimented line.

"You're one of our Malayan group. Good luck to you. You'll maybe need it, the way things are going out there. I was in Burma myself in the second world war."

I had credits. I had signed pieces of paper, that looked very important. I had passed this exam and that. It absolved me from the preliminary examination. It absolved me from the Pre-registration. It absolved me from chemistry and physics and biology, for had I not travelled to Edinburgh for that? I was starting well up the ladder. God help me! He hoped that I was used to it all by this. I knew myself not used to anything very much in the medical line, except what I had picked up on the mountain above Glenmore.

Then I was in a great glass-domed room . . . you could not call it room, for the size of it. You came into it through a door and there was a box office, where you were supposed to clock in, when you started Practical Anatomy.

This was school again with people moving up and down and hither and thither. It brought back the memory of St Mary Peter's, where we had moved in lines, that paused politely for seniority. Strange faces now, all strange faces and the same Tower of Babel quality, that I knew so well. There was not much pausing for good manners here. You made your way along, where you thought you should go. I seemed to find myself in a queue again and then I was through a door and out through another door to stand by a box office window in turn, for this was the heart of the Royal College. Here was the anatomy room and I looked at the tables and the high stools and the benches along the walls, the black tanks that contained God only knew what and over it all the smell of formalin. I was to get so used to it but now it stung the eyes and assaulted the nostrils and I looked away quickly again.

"Stuart, Virginia," I said when my turn came and the porter behind the desk had a dun coat and white hair and a look of an old soldier about him. There was a personal element here. It seemed impossible in such a vast place, but this was Ireland.

"Your mother was a McLean and we had her grandpappy here. Robert McLean he was and a fine wing-three quarters. You'll have come from his son, who is Dr McLean of Glenmore, they tell me, but he's Edinburgh. Edinburgh University."

He might have known me all my days for the friendly way he had.

"You'll want a white coat, Doctor. It won't be white very long."

Now for the first time, I was called 'Doctor', where I was no doctor at all. I was the greenest of medical students and I had no knowledge whatever of surgery or medicine or of midwifery. That was all in the future. Suddenly I was terrified by the thought of it. There was so much knowledge to acquire, so much hard work and exams, that appeared like jumps before a steeple chaser in the Grand National, barriers so enormous that one might as well try to breast the stars.

I had a list of text books I must get, but the done thing was to buy them second hand. It seemed that they were on a par with the white coats. They were not white for long either, nor were they expected to be.

I wandered along Grafton Street and searched the book shelves and got what they had listed for me. Then I found a shop that sold cakes and there was a higher level to it and another level higher again and glass-topped tables everywhere . . . people having coffee, or tea, or ices or cream buns. The whole air was impregnated with the smell of coffee. They must be students, these young people, who came and went in groups and lounged carelessly round in twos or threes. There were so many young people, that it was any ice cream parlour in Kuala Lumpur and there was a wonderful atmosphere to it, for all their zest of living. The waitresses were having a job to keep them in order. I felt lonely and shut out and knew that never would I be able to walk up the stairs, as if I were in my own home and greet so many friends. For the first time, in Ireland, I felt the chill wind of loneliness. I walked through the streets and found the text books heavy to carry. There was a butcher's shop at last and I bought two lamb chops, thickly cut. Suzy had promised to get away that evening and come to supper. We had potatoes in store already and I planned chop and chips, with small cakes to follow and a pot of good coffee. She would have had a heavy day at the hospital and the thought of seeing her to exchange news kept my spirits from flagging, kept the loneliness at bay. The books were heavy under my arm and it was a good walk to the flat, but on the way I found a green park with a lake of ducks and I fed them some of the fresh bread I had bought, just to make some friends. I understood the feeling of being alone in a crowd. Then I had reached the flat and there was pride in putting my key in the lock and letting myself into the square hall. The two ladies greeted me and asked me how I had got on at the College. There were some letters, which had come for me. I carried my post up the stairs to the flat and put it on the draining board with the chops and the cakes and the bread. Then I set the gas poker alight and got the coal fire going in the sitting room. I looked out of the window but I knew there would be no hope of Suzy coming so early. I rifled through the text books, but saw the mile stones of previous travellers in the margins. I would have to get the knowledge transferred from the books to my brain, but this was for tomorrow. There must be something to do to occupy my loneliness, for now I had taken to thinking of Grandfather coming home to an 'empty' house and missing me as much as I missed him. I had scanned the letters and there was nothing of importance so I thought I must pass the time till Suzy's coming by making an exotic supper. I had the chops. I had curry. I had rice and it took a long time to prepare, but at last, it was ready, but the night was coming down. It would keep in the oven for a while so I did not worry. She might be late and time went on. I was back in Malaya, mourning for my parents with the thought that never any more would I arrive at the bungalow to the north of Kuala Lumpur.

I argued to myself that I was a new girl. In a month, I would have got used to Ireland and some of the faces must be familiar. It was just this school syndrome all over again and I must inevitably accept it.

There was a tap at the door and a letter handed in to the kitchenette landing, by one of the small, brittle, twittering ladies.

"I'm sorry, Miss Stuart, but the little nurse can't get away tonight. It's not permitted. She'll come tomorrow, for they've given her a few hours off then and she'll make sure to see you. She came across at lunch-time. We forgot to tell you. She said to say it's not as bad as she thought it would be. She was wearing her uniform and she looked a picture, but then they all do. That blue cloak with the red lining is lovely and the white butterfly cap on her dark hair. She's the prettiest little creature."

She went down the stairs and paused, but the old ladies were past remembering things too well.

"Oh and there's that English stamped letter for you. Liam came back with it after you came home. He missed it out when he came with the second post."

I looked down at the letter and recognised the hand, turned the envelope and saw a crest on the back of it, thanked the old lady and took myself back into solitude and knew the horror of loneliness for I had an evening and a night to spend, completely alone in a strange place and I had a fire in the grate and a table set for a guest. I wanted my mother. I wanted my father. I wanted Grandfather and Janet and Suzy Chan, but there was nothing to do except look through the window at the hospital and wonder what Suzy was doing, thinking, feeling; I seemed to have lost appetite for my supper. I had the letter, but I could find little interest in it. I wanted to go to bed and sleep and wake up with the time past, to start all over again. Instead I took the letters and went through the ones that had already arrived and there was nothing to cheer me, just an invoice for furniture, that was on its way to Dublin, just a sheaf of information that I already knew about the Royal College, just an advertisement from one of the small shops opposite, that they had a sale, starting in a week or two.

I wrote off supper. I sat moodily in front of the coal fire with my legs curled under me and I ran my thumb along the flap of the crested envelope. What could Gareth Grant have to say to me? I had last seen him topping the hill silently as a cloud shadow on his way out of Glenmore and with an air about him that he was glad to be rid of me and my affairs for good. I wondered what small end he had not tied, that must now be tied. The postmark was Cambridge and it had been two days on its way. I wondered if it had flown in by Aer Lingus as I had myself, or if it had arrived by train and across the sea. It did not matter. It had got here safely and it was an inert thing. It could never know homesickness. It might fulfil a purpose and then it would be waste paper. I should have known better. I completely forgot the sharp lesson I had already learned, that things outlive people — that things can acquire an importance surpassing the importance of people. I even forgot the mightiness of the pen above the sword for I was only a foolish young girl, sick for home, like Ruth, who had 'stood breast high amid the alien corn'.

4

The Letters

THIS was not written on the flimsy stuff of Air Mail, but I remembered the letter, that had come from him before, with the post mark of Kuala Lumpur on the envelope. I had it still, tucked away with the two locks of hair, in my jewel box and I knew it by heart. It was strange the way this started with much the same words. He could not have remembered it, but I did.

'Dear Virginia, it's a peculiar thing how I never think of you, but I conjure up the memory as you were that day on the sea wall.

'As you will see, I am safe back in Cambridge, in my same set of rooms on the staircase, looking down on the peace of the cloisters. Outside, of course, as you have leeches and mosquitoes and monsoons, we have traffic, that jams the streets, teeming crowds, that shoulder their way and I long for Slievenailra, where the roads have that green track of sanity running along the centre, where the white line will be painted soon if we don't watch out.

'I have the longing for home tonight and I thought of you. You'll have arrived in Ireland by now and Suzy will have been starched into her uniform. The Royal College could be a strange place and no face that you know. I just want you to remember that, if you need a friend, you have a most sincere one in me. Come to me. Send for me.

'Do not be frightened of the temples of learning. You'll take them by storm. If you liked the Snake Temple at Penang at the age of eight "nothing is blind to you", as they say in Ireland. If you have time, in that heavy schedule of academy, they'll set out for you, write and tell me how it goes.

'As for Cambridge the glory has departed. It's not obligatory to wear gowns although the bicycle is still as popular as your rickshaws. You come up here to get your "pairchment" as Janet would call it, but these days, there is fierce competition. It's not just a leisurely life any more and there is a dearth of the school-grey suit and the collar and tie. It has all gone casual and Father says that even "the college servants" are ashamed of some of the students. He does not appreciate hair styling for the male animal.

'Father will never quit his fortress on Turnish. Mother runs off to London, when she can escape the duties, that keep her at home. She has not been well recently and I often think she pines for Bond Street.'

He signed himself 'GRANT' in the same flamboyant way, but he was in no way ostentatious. I knew that he possessed a fierce pride and later, I came to know that he had cause for such pride. Even when I read that first letter to Dublin, I well realised that he had cause for pride, of birth and breeding, of accomplishment, of behaviour and of humanity too, for what he had done to help myself, whom he hardly knew. Me, he had helped beyond all the call of duty, with no consideration for his own comfort and it was strange how he continued to help me.

Just then, we started a correspondence between us, that had something in common with the letters I had exchanged with my grandfather, when I was a child in Malaya. He was given to illustrating the margins with line drawings too, which was an extraordinary coincidence. Yet that day, I looked at the prideful 'Grant' and thereafter addressed him as Grant.

I have the letters still and will never part with them. His I kept, his to me. Mine to him came into my possession many many years later and they lie in the same mahogany cabinet and will go to the generations to come in the Islands, so that the young people will know what went on between Slievenailra and myself and what honour, they owe to his name.

I take the desk out now and I rifle through the letters and here I pick one and there I pick one, and read our communications one to the other over those important years, that we thought were the most important in life and perhaps they were, but there was a future, that maybe transcended the present.

Here was one from me to him, when I had finished my first year in the Anatomy room.

'Grant,

'Thank you for your letter last week and I am unable to say how much I grieve for you. You say that you understand for the first time, what it was for me when I lost my mother, because you know it now for yourself. It is a tearing out of the roots of the heart and you must not have this guilt feeling that you never understood why she could not settle in Scotland. She was London born and London bred. How could she take to that wild fortress, where the eagles soar, waiting for the Laird to return? There are importances and importances.

'You did not understand this love of London Town and now you are going to do penance in guilt, for sin, that you in no way committed. You have chosen Fleet Street and you intend to tear the world apart and report on what you find amiss, just to wash some imaginary guilt out of your soul.

'If you take to being a foreign correspondent, I will read your articles

136

with interest. Only don't forget the peace of the lovely silent Hebrides and how the salmon come up the burns and how sweet the wild roses are and how peaceful the small roads and how the voices lilt poetry and how that's where you and maybe I belong.

'As to news of Suzy, in less than two years, she will be a trained State Registered Nurse. No doubt they will want her on the staff, so she may eventually be known by the title of "Staff" and wear a black belt like a Judo expert. She insists on waiting for me. She comes to the flat every moment she can and very often, we turn the place over, as if we were spring-cleaning. She does not trust me to keep everything clean and I declare, she makes a god of the old gas oven. I never have it quite right. I spend too much of my time entertaining and she is severe about this.

'I have a year to make the First Professional, but it is like learning the Family Bible off by heart, this Gray's Anatomy. I have studied unmentionable things, but I have human weakness. In Anatomy, the face and neck is the pons asinorum or so I put it to you. You start off on a leg or an arm, dead arm, with a hazy idea in the back of your mind that far in front of you, lies the real stuff of medicine and surgery, and midwifery.

'God have mercy! Enough of this. I am supposed to be cheering you up.

'Suzy is her own mistress and mistress of her fate. She knows where she is going and she knows who's going with her and she sends her felicitations to you . . . and so do I . . . '

There was a final medical student, who as they say in Ireland "had hearts" for Suzy Chan. He was far more senior than I and he was walking the wards. There was romance in the ward kitchens at night, but Suzy was not to be taken lightly. She knew her plans. He might be permitted to come to the flat some afternoons and we took tea together and he and I got on famously. Suzy was very proper with him, but it seemed that Chinese marriages were rather a business matter between parents and love had little part in marriage, yet he adored her with his eyes and they were a strange, small, neat couple, anxious only to do the work they had come to do, with perhaps little thought of romance on the journey. I got a strange premonition of disaster about them. She was Butterfly all over again and I could feel no joy in the thought of happiness for their future. I knew she would fulfil her destiny and that was as far as I could go. As for me, I took romance where it appeared, but with no depth to it. There was no dearth of partners, but there was no depth to any emotion I felt. In a strange sort of way, I was faithful to Grant, with no excuse in the world for it. When I thought of falling in love, no, love is too strong a word, when I felt infatuation and very often I felt it, I would remember the depth of him, of Slievenailra's son and the way he wrote to me such letters of wisdom — and matched against him, they were faded candlelight against the sun and so the letters went on.

I pick out another at random and remember it, as if it had just arrived.

'My Lady of the Black Velvet Bow,' so he called me — and I might have just opened it and read . . . and just towards the end.

'Now you're past the First Professional. My most sincere congratulations! You have the hospital to walk and you are set for reality and there is reality — not this crazy world of Fleet Street. I have been sent out to Vietnam . . .

'Here is a country torn in two and north against south and no love for the foreign devils, who interfere. There are shoe shine boys. There are girls wanting nylons and getting them at high experience and a nation turned beggars, for the white man's plenty — and a swift hard enemy, that must surely win — and the old paddy fields, that you are familiar with and the dry season and the only creature happy the ox, that chews its cud and wanders where it listeth, that is loosed in the paddy fields after harvest so that it can fertilise the land and that's about the only sensible thing I have seen here, this rotation of nature. I am not enamoured with Indonesia, with Vietnam nor yet with Cambodia. Here is a tide, that could sweep the face of the world, yet words I write and more words, words, and I appear on BBC with a microphone in my hand and speak to the nations and know that my words are seeds sown on barren ground.

'Why cannot we live at peace with our neighbours and have a dram together, or dance at betrothals or weddings and lead the simple life? Why cannot the world's roads be stitched with a line of grass, and why cannot the old be revered and not forestalled by a colour TV in the corner? Why? Why? Why? What is so important as the emblem of power? Surely it is better to walk the hills, taste the salt of the sea? Surely it is better to catch a trout fresh from the burn and grill it over a small hot fire and eat it with fingers, walk back home down the mountain to the place of one's birth? . . .

'My Lady of the Black Velvet Ribboned Hair, there is such a storm starting here, that will sweep the skies and now is the time to cry halt, and they only throw petrol on fire.'

And mine to him . . .

'Dearest Grant, I do not understand how life makes us move like chessmen on a board and miss each other in passing. I find your letters keep me in your life, yet how am I to be part of your life, when I have not seen you for so many years?

'The hospitals are upon me and I am what they call a clinical clerk and that means that I must see patients in life and not die with them, but regard them as cases, people with wives and husbands, with children and mothers and fathers, yet I cared on the hill of Glenmore and how can I turn off caring like a tap and say "it's only a case" and we have a pride in our non-involvement, God help us medical students, otherwise they tell us we will never survive.'

The letters came through sporadically, now, sometimes in batches of two or three. I read the news, watched television and knew he was in the unhappy country, wandering about, with a camera man and a microphone and too sensitive a mind. He spelt it out for the world and the media chattered his voice across the air, and sometimes I watched him and I knew, or thought I knew, that there was that, between him and me, which would never die. I wrote my letters to him and wished that I could sit in the bracken with him, on a hill and watch the eagles hang high in the sky, but they did so no longer. I had faith that they would come back again, when Grant came home, but his father was dead, suddenly with no warning. It was Grant's duty to come home, but he was out of reach of civilisation, caught up in the prison of a battle arena, that was none of his business, except that no man is an island.

My grandfather had been to the funeral, but there is no point in writing out sorrow here.

I wrote to Grant regularly and said what I could to help him and knew the letters arrived or did not arrive in the foreign land, where the enemy was unbeatable. I saw through his eyes the small boys who had taken to shoe shining for a dime. I saw their sisters taken to intimate fraternising and presently would pay dearly for their nylons. This was a country, which had been invaded and turned upside down, with every value a false one. A great nation had sown generosity and was certain to garner ingratitude, but they had done what they thought right, but maybe it had all turned wrong for them and the blood of their sons was being shed . . . maybe to no purpose! They were going to harvest ingratitude, these generous people, for there was a tide of war running, big enough to involve the whole world once again. There was news to be gathered and broadcast like seed. He knew it well, did Grant, and he showed it to the civilised world, bullet by bullet, word by word, crouched in the front line sometimes, with a straw hat tilted on the back of his head and his smile careless and his shirt open at the neck and sweat stained, a pride on him, that would never be conquered. Yet the British Raj had been conquered jungle battle by jungle battle, and I knew unhappiness, and in the night I had awful nightmares, that woke me with screams choked in my throat, how they were holding him in a prison in a tropic climate, a prison where he could not stand upright and where the sun beat down all day and where a man might sell his soul for a sip of water in hell. It was strange how I dreamt it as it happened and that was why he had not stood at the grave-side, when they buried his father.

They were flying in surgeons from America, who had never been trained for such a theatre. As for myself, I was in the Rotunda by this, learning midwifery, still attached to the Richmond after surgery and medicine and it was a full life, that was utterly divorced from war, only for the thoughts that haunted me in the night, of how Grant might be learning and far harder than I, that one must not shrink from the unpleasantness of any task, nor one must show fear. Callous was a good word not a bad one. Even if your heart was shaken with dread, it was useless to ask for help.

There was a day, when I wondered why I had not trained to become an actress. Medicine was a profession which called for actors and actresses and kept all emotions private and artificial. There might be an hour between midnight and dawning, when there was space to shed tears for mankind, but by morning the time was gone and there was armour to put on. In some strange way, I knew that Grant and I were akin in our suffering, but mine was by far the less. We exchanged letters. We exchanged experiences. God knows what the political censors made of them, but I think in a way, we exchanged our souls. Yet mine was no suffering compared with his. He had lain in prison, when he should have stood by his father's grave and I knew how he had suffered for that. I did my best to comfort him. Perhaps I did. His letters to me were the safety valve on my little agonies. I hoped that mine to him might help him, and there was a time came when he said they saved his life, but we were deep in love by then and there was a long time to go from the present, when it was likely that never, never would we meet face to face.

'Grant, maybe it's better the way it is and you're some confessor through a screen for me and I'm the same to you. I can talk to you on paper as I have never confided in any other person, not even Suzy Chan.

'Suzy is a Sister now. She says go and they go and come and they come. She has the edge on me, who am just a final medical and no degree. She has a battalion of nurses in command and the blue uniform suits her as well and better, than the print. The cap is superb, like a French concoction, that might sell for a great many francs on the Rue de la Paix. It's just the angle she wears it and the slanted brows and the calmness, that lives in her and perhaps a lion tamer's eye, for a sister must have such a thing. She will marry Ling Hoo, for he worships her. He is qualified now and with a "pairchment" that will give him the power of healing in most of the civilised world. I have no doubt that I am partaking in a great union that will eventually take place. They will marry and there will be lovely Chinese children, all like pretty dolls, but with so much potential to them. Still, just for now, she refuses to say "yes". "Maybe" she says. She's still the old faithful amah, entangled in myself, who am entangled with the final exams.

'I hope you are still not blaming yourself, that you could not come home for Slievenailra's funeral. There was no choice open to you. I have gone on about this at length and if ever a man would understand, the old eagle would. I told you I went over one holiday in Glenmore with my grandfather and left cowslips on his grave and how there were no eagles in the sky, but only that great silence of expectation. They will return and so will you.

'It will all work out, but Grant, I had a child die last night and I am nearly destroyed by the pity of it. He came to us from an orphanage with leukaemia. He found no room in the children's ward so he went into Six — a ward of adult men, who were so good to him. The sand was running down the glass for him and we all knew it and refused to accept it. We turned our eyes away and hoped for a miracle, but miracles are not just yet. Red-headed he was, with false freckles on a white face, aged six, and no more years left to him. He was happy, happy, happy in that ward. I took to the habit of bringing in a Mars bar to him every day and then came the day when a Mars bar had no delight for him and he died with my hand in his. I knew then the price I was paying for this noble career of mine. Why did I not seek the profession of digging ditches? It's forbidden to get involved, but that's your weakness as well as my weakness. Why else would you be out there under the burning glass and the green hills of Turnish calling you home and you not able to quit what you think to be your duty? Why cannot we both take to this sane thing called non-involvement? But Grant, do not fret about the Old Eagle. He was glad when we put the cowslips on his grave and he is well aware that life goes on . . . that soon you will be back . . . that the eagles will nest again. Maybe there's something in paradise to equal the peace of that Hebridean island, though maybe I doubt it, as you doubt it. Just for now, good-bye! God bless you and keep you safe!'

I pass a finger along the letters and know the one that came to tell me he still lived, but that the war was almost certainly lost. They were getting out or would get out soon and then God help the folk, that had been on their side, but it would not be yet for a while. I pass it by. It is all written in history by now and what was in the future must beckon us . . . and I had delivered a baby, my first solo delivery, but not my last.

It was such a busy marvellous life. There was no time to think of anything except approaching examinations, of lectures in the Royal College and ward rounds at the Rotunda and at the Meath and at the Mater and at Jervis Street and at the Adelaide . . . We knew the good clinical lecturers and we knew who our examiners would be. It was very essential to haunt the examiners on their ward rounds and learn their special 'things'. They were highly individualised these powerful learned men.

We worked hard, yet we played hard too. There were tennis courts in most of the Residences and we banged balls across the nets with any energy we had left. There was lacrosse on Wednesday and Saturday afternoons too. The mixed hockey team did bloodier work than any operation in the theatre. There were the dances and the romances, and I fell into love and out again and I still did not find the man for me. I might think at first that I had seen him across a crowded lecture. I might be awed into infatuation by the Professor of Medicine and think that here he had come at last.

The Professor asked me to the Ballet at the Gaiety Theatre and took me back to his house in Fitzwilliam Square. I saw the Chippendale dining room, that doubled as his waiting room and found myself in a comfortable chair before the drawing room fire. He fidgeted with the television and then turned the sound out but not the picture — told me he had two tickets for the Lifeboat Dance in the Gresham Hotel. He was just about to ask me to go with him, when Grant came into the room. It was the strangest thing. There he was on the silent television, standing against a harbour wall somewhere and behind him were craft such as I had known in Malayan days. On land there were people like ants, from an overturned nest. Here was the rout of a lost war. It had happened before, but perhaps never like this. There were whirly birds against the sky, cars and trucks and hand carts, loaded far past the filling, with jetsam people and possessions . . . and no happiness in any face. The camera zoomed down on an old man with a begging bowl, empty white eyes turned up to heaven. Then we were flashed from frame to frame, a mother with her baby on her naked breast and her tears running down the baby's face too, a coolie with a rush basket and the coconuts and bananas and mangoes, it had contained, spilled about him and children fighting over them like dogs. An ancient white bearded man with a staff, in a wide straw hat, who just stood stunned, not able to understand what was happening.

I forgot where I was. Maybe today, I could be wife to that eligible man, the Professor, but for the fact, that I got down on my knees and turned the TV up and brought the real scene to life, for here was Grant, microphone in hand, a straw hat with a striped ribbon tilted over his eyes, his face brown from the sun, but tiredness on him. He was dressed in khaki slacks and a green open necked shirt and there was no consciousness about him that millions of people might be watching him. He must have got used to being international on this media. Yet for me there was nobody in the world but he and I. Yet he could not know that I was one of the millions. How could he have any thought for me?

It was the same voice . . .

"Hello there! Here we are in the city of . . . "

There was a buzzing sound that made the name anonymous, but this was the pattern of foreign news. He was monitored, but they had let him off with his life from that pit prison, because of his international fame. He had prestige and power and respect. He was in a port and there was only one place it could be so what did it matter if they buzzed out the name and presently they were not so careful . . .

"Here then is the end of the swift last campaign of the war. It might be France in 1940 and who could think it could have happened all over here? You know that the first communist attack was on Ban Me Thuat in the Highlands on the tenth of March. On the tenth of April, the Red Flag was run up over the Presidential Palace in Saigon. The Ambassador had just escaped from the roof by helicopter, but here is the end of a great idealism . . . here in South Vietnam. Fifty five thousand men lie dead, and untold billions of dollars have been spent and twenty years are lost, of tremendous effort to uphold the right. It is a high price for idealism, but it was paid — and maybe for nothing.

"There are people being left behind, but evacuation was left too late. Grahame Martin, the Ambassador, turned a blind eye to direct orders from Washington to cease all evacuation. He went on with evacuation, till time was all run out. He wanted to get his people to freedom, but it was a vain attempt. You can see for yourselves what is happening at this very moment in history. The forces of the North have won and are entering the capital city of Saigon. All types of craft are setting out, overloaded and with scant supplies. They have no hope in their faces, probably no future. Their enemy is right behind them and the war is lost. There is gunfire in the streets and soon there will be firing squads . . . and more blood flowing. The United States army have been driven from this land by incompetence in local support and by greed in high places. America took up the burden of the world to fight for right in this far away place. She will never give up her fight for what she considers to be right and true. She will never surrender to the forces, that are threatening to overwhelm the world. She holds the power and the glory and this is just one war, maybe one battle lost, but never the last battle, for the last battle decides who wins a war and this war will be won and America will never cease to aid small people and small nations to escape the invasion of the oppressor.

"This is Gareth Grant, speaking to you from Saigon in South Vietnam signing off now, with the Statue of Liberty in my heart's eye . . . and all that it stands for and will ever so stand . . . "

He was a mature man, this Professor of Medicine far more worldly wise than any of his students. He said nothing till the programme turned to some pop festival recording, that made me realise that we were fiddling while Rome burned. He got up and switched off the ragged clothed youths and their girls with maenad hair styles, switched the jungle rhythm down to a small bright spot, which faded to darkness.

"Of course, you're the Malayan student.

They say you're in love with that chap on the screen just now, that you are old childhood friends. They say . . . they say . . . they say . . . This small medical world is a gossip shop, but I see by your face that maybe there's truth in it. They say you're all set for a crusade to that hospital in Kuala Lumpur. They want you as soon as they can get you. You'll pass your finals of course. You're a bright one. Then you have a year's hospital to fill up, learning the stuff that matters. You'll have to pick up tropical medicine too — it's going to be a deal of hard work. Then ICI wants you soon, as I suppose you're still set on the Federation of Malaya?"

I nodded my head, but I was not in that rich drawing room. I was leaning against the harbour wall beside Grant wondering how he could possibly escape from what was soon to be known as Ho Chi Minh City.

"I'm still set on it."

He put the tickets for the Lifeboat Dance into my hand and told me to use them to give some poor chap a break and I sensed that I was right in thinking he might have asked me to marry him. Perhaps I am wrong, but I do not think I am and now I might be a respectable professional wife living in Fitzwilliam Square but it was all wrong for me and he knew it. He was kind and he thanked me for the pleasure I had given him in accompanying him to the Ballet and he wished me luck on the way to the Far East . . . told me to follow my star, took me home in his car and watched me let myself into the flat in Leeson Street and then sat outside while he finished a cigarette and thought about myself and Grant, for I watched him through the window, till at last he took himself away, with the stub of his cigarette a spark on the dark road.

It was one of those times that sped on swift feet. Soon I was swearing the Hippocratic oath with a number of others, clad in a black gown with a piping of pale blue and the mortarboard on my head. Hippocrates had been a celebrated Greek physician, the father of Medicine, a careful observant man and a strong believer in surgery. His oath was the earliest and most impressive of medical ethics and we stuck to it still . . . and the big board room was packed with relatives come to see us receive the honour of our degree. Grandfather had crossed the Irish Sea and he gave us a celebration dinner that evening in the Hibernian, Suzy Chan, her betrothed, Dr Ling Hoo, and myself. I saw the future stretching out in front of us and no difficulty to come in achieving what we were setting out to do.

I knew that Grant was long safely out of Vietnam. It had been reported in the press, but as yet I had had no letter. In Dawson Street earlier in the evening, Grandfather had surprised me.

"It's a gey strange thing the way you always miss young Grant. He came over to see the grave and you were away on that project in Connaught, but that's a while past. Then when you came home on holidays, he was away. He intended to fly across to see you take your 'pairchment'. It was to be a great surprise for you, and we kept it a close secret. It was as well. All the planes were grounded at Singapore with the bad weather. He sent a cable to call it off — sent you his felicitations. I've known him try to meet you in Glenmore a time or two, but it's just not meant to be. I daresay fate has something special in store and when you do meet, it will be a great moment."

Grandfather had been to the Royal College to see his father's name in gold on the plaque. It was the last thing he did, before he flew off home in the Aer Lingus plane. He had stayed almost a week in the flat and when he had gone, it seemed very empty, but there was no time for loneliness. There was the business of my year as an intern. There was the marriage of Suzy to Dr Ling Hoo. For some reason, he was never called anything but 'Fred' and he was a gentle kind idealist. They were married in a ceremony in some little country church, outside Dublin. Fred called himself 'a Rice Christian'. He was a foundling, brought up in a Mission School in Bangkok and he had no parents to haggle over marriage settlements with Suzy's kin and anyhow, she had no kin. It was all simple . . .

There were some of the Richmond

and the Baggot Street hospital staff there, doctors and nurses, and they made great joy out of it . . . fireworks afterwards, because there must be a Chinese background . . .

Fred was Registrar at the Richmond and I was to be House Physician first and then House Surgeon. Suzy was to stay on part-time in her hospital. I was living in. Suzy and Fred shared the flat together and it seemed that nothing could ever go wrong for us.

They wanted us in Malaya, all three of us in one hospital. Letters flew back and forth, and it all ran too smoothly. Fred was elected Junior consultant in Medicine. I was to be Medical Registrar. Suzy was offered Sister status, senior grade.

I knew the hospital in Kuala Lumpur very well indeed. Had I not had my tonsils out there many years ago?

I had Tropical Medicine to pick up, somewhere along the line. I took a grind from an ancient Medic Chinese philosopher in Rathmines and I passed an exam in Tropical Medicine in London. I had not much confidence that I knew much about the subject, yet the names were familiar enough.

The months sped past. I visited Glenmore every chance I got. Grandfather had retired and was as happy as a king. He followed my career with total involvement. Every week I wrote to him twice and got regular letters back from him with the same old line drawings. When the time was right, on the eve of our departure, we visited Glenmore for a farewell reunion, Suzy and Fred and I. At the last moment, I wanted to cancel all the fine planning and stay there with him, but he laughed me out of that and bade me be on my way. Yet the thought still stuck in my mind how lonely an old man could look in the hall of a Scots airport, standing beside the statue of Robbie Burns, as he had so often stood, waiting for me to arrive after the holidays . . .

Then it was all over, all the farewell sadness and we were boarding the plane at Heathrow, Fred and Suzy and myself. Here was the crowded lounge, but at last, I had my foot on the gangway. There was a van, that tore across the tarmac and

161

pulled up with a scream of brakes. A girl jumped out of the driver's seat, proud of having defied authority. I was almost at the plane door, when the stewardess turned to me. There was a small space, while the girl was allowed up to where I stood to, a sheaf of roses in her arms. The passengers were straining to see if I was a celebrity, but Suzy waved to me from the tarmac to get aboard.

"You needn't be afraid of the thorns, Madam," the florist girl told me and presently I was sitting in my seat aboard and looking at the card that accompanied the roses.

Suzy sat beside me, telling me it was to be a great surprise. She had wondered what had gone wrong, but just now Fred had found out that the planes had been grounded at Kuala Lumpur owing to bad weather conditions . . . days and days of delay . . .

'I planned to fly over and bring you home, but it's not possible. It's not to be and why should this always happen between you and me? "I will see thee at Philippi." Don't doubt it for one moment!'

Then came the typed signature GRANT, that had none of the flamboyance of his own hand . . .

He had thought enough of me to try to come all the way to England to bring me home to Malaya. That was a wonderful fact. He had considered me important enough in his life to be on the road home with me.

5

The Secret State

IT was a wonderful journey. We changed into tropical gear along the way and there was Suzy again in her white starched jacket and black slacks, with the straw hat slung on her back by a thong, the dark eyes gleaming with anticipation, the hair like black satin, the slanted brows. It seemed to me that time had ticked back to that first day, when I arrived in Scotland wearing my school uniform and very uncomfortable, it had been in the tropics. Now I had settled, like Suzy for a pair of black slacks and a white 'wind-cheater', that would in no way cheat the wind, even if I had bought it in Switzers. A loose silk scarf in the neck and a pair of sandals on my bare feet and the old black velvet ribbon in my hair for some superstitious reason . . . and I wondered what Grant would look like at Kuala Lumpur. Might there be a great change in him, for he had had fearful adventures? He had known a prison camp and hunger and thirst . . . a glazing sun and no water. He had known confinement in a little space, guerilla troops, with small civilisation. I remembered him as a young undergraduate. I wondered what the years had made of him and what change he might see in me for perhaps I had changed. I was all scientist and I perhaps had learnt the art of the Snake Temple. I had become an accomplished actress and my heart would never appear on my sleeve. I had fought with death and won. I had fought with death and lost and knew that death always won in the finish.

We were flying Malaya Air Lines and the food was like home again. I had the shrimp curry and all the things that went with it and ate an ice cream concoction nine inches tall, with banana and coconut and mangoes and guava jelly and cinnamon and fresh cream, thick at the top and more chopped coconut . . . and I tasted coffee beans, freshly ground, and made into such coffee that I never remembered and wondered if they had given up the condensed milk, instant coffee that I recalled.

Rice, rubber, tin, tobacco, tea, sugar, quinine, sweet potatoes and nutmegs, I thought to myself — the exports of my country and on the edge of my mind lingered the hill of Glenmore, but it had almost tipped over the rim of the world, with its salmon and pheasants and grouse and the mountain snow caps in winter . . . and the green seas off Scarba . . . and Grandfather and hot scones, that ran butter down your chin . . . and Ireland with the smell of malt and the sweet softness of the voices . . . and the Guinness's barges on the river Liffey running out to the sea . . . and the moan of the Poolbeg light.

We landed and slept in a square concrete house with bunk beds and air conditioning. We took off and continued our journey again and most of the time, we talked shop. I told them what I remembered as a child of the Malayan hospital, but it had been a long time ago. It had not had all the facilities of modern Dublin and there had been the problem of working in the tropics. It would not be difficult for us. We were all used to the heat and the sweat and the lizards and the spiders and the cicadas and the paddy field frogs. Malaya was an emergent country and the population was young. The western world had let itself grow old and in modern times, this included Britain too, just like the Roman and the Greek empires.

Singapore was a state of teenagers and they had no use for the wisdom of age. We were all young and determined to bring about an improvement in the future and the hospital near Kuala Lumpur was the start of it. That was what we had been trained for and that was our aim and we had no inferiority complex about the amount of experience we might or might not have. We were all very young, even Suzy but perhaps she was the wisest of the three of us. We were uppity! Gracious goodness! We were uppity!

There was trouble in Kuala Lumpur airport still, they told us over the loud speaker. There had been a severe storm and damage to the runways, our plane might be diverted to Singapore, but there was no cause for worry. Transport would be provided to convey us with the minimum of delay to the Federation of Malaya. There had been this freak series of severe thunderstorms and it was unusual at this time of the year. It would not be long before the runway repairs were carried out, but there might be a small delay . . . we were going to divert to Singapore. Suzy and Fred and I had got together in the bar of the plane and were drinking tomato juice. We talked shop and more shop and Suzy confided in us that as a trainee at the Rotunda Hospital, she had marched along the line of prams outside the antenatal clinic and taken away the babies' dummies.

"They drop them on the floor and straight away, they are back in the mouth and the germs grow and multiply. 'But the baby cries and cries,' they tell me. Me, I like to hear a baby cry, it is when it is not crying that I fear. I say 'Beware a silent baby, for it may never cry again,' but they buy more dummies and put them in the childrens' mouths and they laugh at the chinky, chinky, Chinese sister, that has such foreign ideas . . . only they remember to put the dummies in their purses and not leave them outside the Rotunda Hospital in the pram queue any more . . . "

There was another click from the tannoy.

"The electric storm seems to have spread south to Singapore. They are not accepting planes for landing. They have had no departures or landings for twenty four hours and the airport is crowded with stranded passengers. We are changing our course now, north back along the route we have travelled. We will land at the most suitable base and await favourable conditions and then try for Kuala Lumpur again."

The Captain came along the plane and stopped and spoke to us. We were going to reduce height and when we were through the cloud barrier, we would see the peninsula of Malaya on the port side. There was a deal of water below, which could only be the South China Sea and I imagined he was making for Bangkok. I felt uneasy because he was flying low. I sensed there was something amiss. Maybe his Radio communication was on the blink. I recognised the east coast of Malaya. Then after a while, he had veered off and the engines were starting to stutter a bit. Then there was land to the starboard. I saw the fingers of a delta. I knew the map well. It could only be the Mekong Delta, a huge area, veined with waterways, all running down to the sea in a triangle, a swamp in the rainy season, but that was not yet. There was flat land to the north west and that was the 'Secret State', the loneliest place in the world . . . flat, flat, flat. The engine was missing again and the click of the tannoy came.

"We have engine trouble. It never rains but it pours. Not to worry! We'll put down as soon as we get clearance. It's only as a precaution that we ask you to stay in your seats to fasten your safety belts and to extinguish all cigarettes."

"That's Democratic Kampuchea down there," Suzy said.

"There's big trouble. The borders are sealed and refugees are trying to get out. Did you see it on television last week?"

There was an air hostess leaning in to speak to us.

"Permit that I verify the fact that

you're two doctors and a nursing sister? It's confidential, but we may have to make an emergency landing. It's best that you know."

We were fastening our safety belts and we nodded at her.

"Is good, but I hope we will not need your help. Is flat terrain, on the border between Vietnam and Cambodia."

It all happened so quickly. The tannoy clicked on again and the Captain's voice was carefree enough.

"We seem to have hit Radio interference, so we must run in very low. We are crossing the border into Vietnam now. It's as flat as an air strip. I think we will land soon."

He must have forgotten to turn off the intercom to the plane and presently we heard a very different tone in his voice and now native Malay and high with apprehension.

"There is ground fire . . . men in battle-dress and with automatic rifles. There's a helicopter on our port wing. I can see the gun turrets firing."

The voice clicked off suddenly, but we had understood what he said and no doubt many of the passengers had too. There was a wave of agitation, that swept the whole passenger compartment, as a wind shakes a field of barley. One of the hostesses appeared up front with a microphone in her hand, smiling.

"Do not move from your seats and see to those safety belts. I think we land now and then the escape hatches will go out. You will slide down the chutes, like in a fun fair and when you land, leave the command to the Captain. There are people here, who may not like us."

It was the assassination of John Kennedy all over again, but we were such small unimportant people. Fred was sitting with us, with Suzy next to him, his hand in hers. There was a sharp scatter of breaking glass and Fred slumped down and Suzy gathered him into her arms. There was a starred hole in the window — and another. Fred had a bullet in his head and a second in his neck and his life was running away, was gone. There were no body-guards to help and no hospital — only Suzy crouching over him and the plane running lower. The kampongs were a child's toys and then bigger and bigger, but no trees. I could not understand that there were people, who might think it a noble thing to kill Fred, poor, gentle Fred. Suzy's jacket was soaked with his blood. His head was in her lap and the first bullet had shattered his brain, the second his carotid and all the side of his neck. I opened my safety belt and took off my wind cheater and tried to wrap the wounds as best I could and Suzy was out of her safety belt too, to get more freedom to move. Fred still lolled sideways but he was dead and I knew that there was no use for hospital. There was no reality about any part of it. Our wheels had touched down and the plane was running fast along the ground. There were men in peaked hats and each of them with an automatic rifle at his hip. I saw them in the failing light, saw the flashing of their fire. We blundered along the ground and our undercarriage was collapsing. We slid along to a grinding stop and the night was almost upon us. The escape hatches were open and two of the hostesses were standing, braced against the hand rails. My mental speed changed tortoise. I was completely disorientated. There was

173

a great blast of noise and I was flung into space and all the time was the sound of gun-fire. It was very hot. I had the consciousness to recognise the tropical humidity. I was in a clump of bamboo. I lay there, stunned. Then Suzy's hand was clasping mine and I thought it might be a mercy if she were dead . . . if I were dead too. Yet we were kneeling to peer through the bamboo leaves at what was happening to the plane.

It was a hell holocaust, blazing to the skies, yet some of the passengers had managed to escape and were running round like rats, hither and thither, darting, staggering, being hunted and gunned down and the soldiers feeding their bodies back into the flames. At last they came to search and I dragged Suzy along through the bamboo away from the fire. We stumbled through the darkness, away from the light. She struggled with me, for she wanted to go back.

"There's nothing we can do. He's in paradise."

At last, she gave in and came with me, but she was like a dead woman.

"We weren't saved for nothing, Suzy.

If they find us, they'll kill us too, as they killed the others, harmless people, only us two left and none of our happiness."

There was a great anger that possessed me and the fact that we were powerless made it no less and Suzy had flame from me and made as if to go back again.

"There's nothing for me here. They killed him. I'll find a gun and I'll take some of them with me."

She turned and ran and I went after her and brought her down in a tackle, held her down by force and whispered to her, dried her face for there were tears now. Our clothes had been blown to tatters in the blast and I remember that I used a small fragment of my scarf to dry her tears and I whispered to her with fierceness, till presently she lay quiet in my arms.

"Not now, Suzy, not now. We live to come back another day. It's bad here. We must put distance between us and them. We move now and the night will hide us. In darkness, we move and lie up by day. Come!"

We came to a paddy field at the edge of the bamboo and Suzy was her old

175

inscrutable self by this time. Our feet were bare. We were in tattered black slacks and the remnants of white shirts. So, we walked along through paddy field country and I thought to myself that it might be easy enough to pass ourselves off as two destitute Chinese women. The paddy fields were familiar enough to us from Malaya and when the rains came, this would be a green fertile plain, with the croaking of the frogs in the swamps. Just now, it would be golden brown for the dry season. By day, it would be a burning glass. Sometimes, as we went, we came across an upturned boat and the drying racks for the fish and the nets. It seemed that everything waited the coming of the water. We found a river and drank deeply, filled an old army canteen, we had found to bring a supply of water with us and we were not able to speak, for silence had come down between us and it was a bad thing. We moved through an empty night in a country without people. There were no villages and no soldiers. We travelled at the best speed we could make and the land was very flat still. By the morning, we had reached another small stream, where somebody had built a ramshackle shed on the bank. A water buffalo left his grazing of the dried rice straw and came to shake his horns at us and at the flying insects, that had started to torment him. The shed was his, we thought, but he allowed us to share it. We wanted no food, only water. We slept with intervals of frightful dreams and in the afternoon we awoke again, plaited river reeds into round shady hats . . . went to wash in the river with what clothes we possessed still on . . . dried in five minutes in the heat of the day. We kept look-out in the last hours of the sun and there were very few people on the move. There were a few helicopters patrolling the skies. Back in the direction of the plane crash, there was still gun-fire. I began to worry about Grandfather and Grant. The news of the missing plane must have leaked out by now. Grant would be at Kuala Lumpur and he might come looking for us. In Glenmore, it was all so remote. They must know everybody had been killed or imply it, but this was a strange secret place. There was war on the border of Vietnam and Cambodia and presumably we had come down in No-Mans' Land. Who was to report what had happened? We might just have vanished into nothingness, and it was time for us to walk on through the night again, but now we talked bravely and tried to lift our spirits, even discussed the old days in Malaya and the ice cream towers we had eaten in Kuala Lumpur. In our minds we went back to our medical student days, but Fred was shut out. Fred was gone, closed from our minds in a tremendous sense of loss.

In the middle of the night, we came on a potato field and dug some with our hands and ate them raw. We found fish drying on racks and ate them, as they were. Then the day was coming and we rested again and waited and so it went on and all time lost to us.

One evening, we came to a kampong with palm leaf houses on stilts, with men and women, who kept pigs. They thought us beggars. There was an old man on a veranda, an old Chinese, with white shirt and black trousers and a wide straw hat, which I coveted very much.

I put my hands together in the praying gesture and spoke Mandarin Chinese to him and he listened to me and went off and came back presently with the old men of the village. They believed what I had said. They knew that a plane had been shot down, but if they helped us, they would be killed. People would come from across the border and kill them and us. We might think we had travelled a long way, but we had walked in circles. Then Suzy told them about Fred.

The women gathered about us and gave us bowls of rice and fish.

"Man can live without a roof and walls, but not without a daily bowl of rice," the first old man said.

They were sad for our sorrow and they lit joss sticks before a statue and we thought that this was sending up some prayer for Fred too and we were comforted.

The conference went on for a long time and there were those that were for and those against.

I hardly think we realised the courage of what the old man intended to do for us. They supplied a Convent Mission

Hospital with rice and fish. Once the nuns had taken him in, when he was very ill, years ago and all the payment, they had asked from him was that he remember them in his prayers. One day in every week, one of the young men of the village took the buffalo cart to the Convent. It had gone on a long time and people were well accustomed to seeing the rice, and the fish being taken to the Mission. The nuns prayed to a foreign god and they came from the other side of the world, but they were laughing always and they would not let a man die, till his time had come. In three days now, the cart was due to travel and we might travel with it, deep in rice straw and no man the wiser. Mother Paul would take us in and she would see that we came to no harm. She would comfort the little Chinese lady, who had lost her man and maybe there would be work for a nurse's hands to do, to make the sorrow less . . . and as for a doctor . . . the nuns had no doctor. No doubt it was the fact that they had prayed for one and I had arrived. Their God was a foreign god, but what did it matter? We would lie hidden securely from men's eyes, not tomorrow and not the day after, but the day after that . . .

The day we left I tried to thank him. The nuns would shelter us and he was risking his whole village.

"Confucius says that 'while you cannot serve man, how can you serve the spirits'?" he replied and his face was a parchment, wrinkled and aged. He had given us shelter and new cotton shirts and black cotton trousers and thonged sandals and I knelt down before him, bent my head and kissed his hand, and thought that his bones were like a bird's bones.

"If ye be kind to women and fear to wrong them, God is well acquainted with what ye do," I quoted to him and he smiled at me and gave me the universal code of all gods.

"Is nothing," he said. "What ye do not like when done to yourselves do not unto others and I am calling on Confucius again, but you speak from the Koran and you are the strangest mem I ever saw, young white-haired woman."

"I believe in one God and I believe

181

that all gods are one God ... " I said and got to my feet and made a deep bow to him, for woman is a lowly creature here.

Then Suzy and I were deep in rice straw and the day hot almost past bearing. The sweat ran down our bodies and soaked our clothes, but there would be the Mission Hospital soon to look forward to, where we could wash and get a good meal. Above all, we would be safe, safe, safe, and we able to earn our keep in Vietnam. It was a hospital and it had saved the old man's life. What we wanted was hard work and forgetfulness, and to lie hid, like a bird on its nest. The nuns, would probably be French. This had been French Indo-China.

The cart jolted slowly along and we met no soldiers to question us. The baskets of fish and the plastic bags of rice were undisturbed. The night was coming down, when Joseph, the driver, told us we were nearly there, we thought of the cold bath of water and the delicious food, convents always seem to have for visitors, and the welcome too, the luxury of a mat on the floor to sleep and another day and tomorrow and safety. We knelt up and shook off the straw, that had covered us and I wondered why we had not imagined the possibility of there being no town.

"Only the nuns' Temple is left," Joseph said. "Even their hospital is gone, the place where their Christ made men walk again."

The village was the bombed ruin of any village. All that remained was a white concrete building with a cross askew on the east wall of it.

"There was a battle here. Mother Paul took in the soldiers and she is a very good woman. She would turn nobody from the door . . . said that the pass-word was sickness or wounding or death. She is a far-seeing mem, but she is very old. She looks into heaven now. They all do. They're old, the holy sisters. They know it's gone . . . has been gone a long time. It will not be necessary for you to tell them what had happened. My brother ran here yesterday, so that they would get ready against our coming at darkness tonight . . . "

They were hurrying out to greet us and

not one of them younger than sixty. They must indeed have been in battle for their white habits were disreputable past any nursing standard. There was an old sister with a sculpted face and dignity, but her sleeves rolled up to the elbow. She had a smile stitched to her lips and apology in her eyes, yet there was calm all about her and I did not rightly see how it came about, but she had gathered Suzy into her arms.

"God comfort you, my daughter. I wish we were in Cork or in Limerick or even in Banagher on the banks of the River Shannon. There's no time for to welcome you, but know that your life isn't at an end, Acushla. There's a task for you to do and hardly an hour, till it must be started."

She spun round on Joseph and told him to throw down his load and turn the beast's head back the way we had come.

"Get away, Joseph and our thanks to you . . . but go home now." The other nuns were pushing a loaded hand cart near the wagon and were packing in the bag of rice and the basket of fish. Then they were piling straw on top of it and all I could think of was that they spoke with the voice of Ireland. Of course, they were Irish nuns. There were Irish nuns everywhere, all over the world.

"Go now, Joseph, and our blessings go with you, but make haste. They're coming in from the border and they're not half an hour away . . . and they're murdering devils, without mercy."

Joseph tried to thank her, because she blessed him but she pushed him away.

"Hurry! Hurry! Hurry!"

Then she put a hand in the pocket of the disreputable habit.

"For you, Joseph. I made some little iced cakes today but don't wait to eat them. Take a stick to that animal if you must and get clear of us — and God keep you safe in the hollow of His hand."

Here was Mother Paul indeed and she had picked me out for who I was and was taking me through to the shelter of the building. We were in the Chapel, I saw Christ crucified again too — in bright colours on the near wall, saw the rough wood benches and the waiting congregation huddled there.

185

"Maybe you're thinking that you drew them down on us, the soldiers and God pity them, but we brought the trouble on ourselves and I've no time to explain it to you, only to tell you that we couldn't shut the door against women and children." I looked at a young girl, heavy with child, who was praying in front of a statue, and the statue might have been smashed by Cromwell and still I could not understand what had happened, only that a great tragedy was being enacted, as I watched — and that it was something far greater than any of us, and would be played to the bitter end.

"I'll have to tell you quickly. It's not wise to write it down. Sister Mary thought we should have written a list, but I'll tell you and you'll tell no mortal person, only keep it close in your own head." Her voice was a whisper in my ear and her hand steadied my arm.

She wasted no time in giving me an inventory, explaining first that here was a party of people that Suzy and I must smuggle out to what safety we could find. We had come through a plane crash and we had escaped fire and battle. We could do it again and the Almighty had preserved us to do it again, when nobody else was at hand — like Abraham making the sacrifice and the lamb that was in it, caught in the thicket?

"Jenny there, she's one of our probationers, fresh out from Ireland and her husband killed in war there . . . and no word out of her that she's expecting a baby. We've dressed her up in a sari and she'll pass, and the children have camouflage too." A smile was a ghost that haunted her lips . . .

"Those three little girls. We call them Elsie and Lacie and Tillie . . . "

"They lived in the bottom of a well . . . a well of treacle," I said, and she approved that I knew my Mad Hatter's Tea Party from Alice and maybe her heart lifted a little.

"They're the daughters of an Oil Sheik. They lived in the lap of luxury and what they wanted, they had, but not now! They're worth three million pounds ransom between them."

She looked at me briefly and went on again.

"They're spoilt rotten, but that's no

reason for letting them have their throats cut, the minute the ransom is paid up, for that's what they'll do. I know my enemy. Next them, that boy with the big glasses on his nose. He's knee high to a grasshopper and that's what we call him . . . 'the Little Grass-Hopper'. His father owns the top right half of Scotland or maybe the top left half . . . anyway it's all grouse moors, but he's a good little fellow. I'd like to think you make it possible for him to be Laird one day, but it's a labour of Hercules I'm putting on your shoulders and if only there was the time to tell you the whole of it. If only our little hospital was resurrected again and now we'd have a doctor and a sister and the work we could have done for God — but it's not to be . . . and I'm wasting precious time in dreaming."

"Don't worry, Mother Paul. We'll get by."

There was a schoolboy as like the young Eaglet of Slievenailra as two peas in a pod, that day at the Scots airport and he tried to comfort Mother Paul and knew that she was preparing to die, when I had no idea of it . . . and that other day, he had wound the long scarf round Suzy . . . Mother Paul tucked her arm into his and told me he was her 'Great Councillor'.

"I call him 'Gordonstoun'. It's enough for you to know, in case it goes wrong. His father was at the British Embassy and we have no news of his people. This lot arrived here in an army lorry and they were given into our care for safe keeping, but there was a leak of information. We could have kept them as safe as lambs in the haggard, but they came to know what we had hidden here. Tonight at the latest we'll give an account of our stewardship."

The picture fell into place like a solved jig-saw. Here were the children of people like Suzy and myself, like Suzy's husband, caught up in a border war. Even poor pregnant Jenny had been caught up in another border war. I was to be in charge of 'Operation Pied Piper'. There was no time to spare to say yes or no. My plans had been made for me and the cart packed and Joseph was safe away. The nuns helped us load the last things on the handcart, helped to push it to the gates with Jenny riding on a heap of blankets with a bag of rice on her lap.

Suzy had not spoken from start to finish. She had stood at my right hand and listened and she might have been any nursing sister from a top hospital, taking regulation orders from the day staff.

She spoke at last and it was to ask permission to stay behind in the Convent with the nuns, but she bowed her head to the refusal.

"Dr Stuart will have need of you, not us. We have nothing more to give and please you must hurry, hurry, hurry."

Mother Paul's voice was urgent and there was lightning on the horizon and presently the sound of the thunder of guns. The children had been lined up to walk behind the cart and we pushed it as quickly as we could . . .

I had been expecting a hospital in South Vietnam where Suzy and I could work and forget. I was lost in time and space and I had not grasped the full situation. We were in border country still . . .

"Now we'll go into the chapel and we'll say Benediction and perhaps there will be time enough to sing a hymn," Sister Paul said. Indeed we heard it, half a mile up the track away, the wheeze of an old harmonium.

'Abide with me, fast falls the eventide,
The darkness deepens, Lord with me
   abide,
When other helpers fail and comforts
   flee,
Help of the helpless, O, abide with
   me.
Swift to its close, ebbs out life's little
   day . . . '

There was something awful just about to happen. We must have been a mile along the retreat route, when the full picture of what it was clicked into my mind like a picture on a screen. I had been tired. I had not realised. If I had known she expected to die, and how could I not have known, never would I have quitted Mother Paul's side. Now I heard the rattle of automatic fire and Jenny was off the cart and was pushing it with all her might.

"There's anger in me, Dr Stuart — maybe anger against heaven. I'd best be pushing the cart a bit. Having a baby's natural and it might stop me from praying men to hell. It's a bad prayer to make to a God of mercy."

If I was in command, I made a poor show of it, but there was Gordonstoun at my side.

"With luck, it will be all over by now and the treacle triplets are giving the Malayan amah a bad time. They want to be carried. I don't think Mother Paul told you about their amah, her name is Raihana and she's not able to cope with the oil heiresses . . . and please stop crucifying yourself that we didn't stay on there. Don't think that I'm not having hell thoughts myself, but we did the only possible thing."

"They will come after us along the trail."

Even the 'Grass-hopper' was wiser than I, this small boy with owl-spectacles and his head tilted because of some defect in his vision. In-breeding, I thought, and a droop to his eyelids and a too big head. Here was a potential Churchill, aged about eight, his hand creeping into mine.

"I think that maybe we should take

cover," he whispered and I spotted the kampong against the sky-line and we made for it. It was no good to hide in the stilt house itself. We found a shed of straw and we pushed the handcart into it and covered ourselves over with golden rice straw. We lay low and silent and 'Hopper' at my side was confidential about his misery and I held him close.

He was six not eight. His home was far away. He thanked me very politely for doing my best to smuggle him to Scotland. He had been in the Convent Mission, just for safety and he was too polite to ask me how long it would be till I got him safe home, if ever. His parents had not sent him his hamper from Fortnum's. He thought it might be impossible because of the state of the country, and Scotland was a long way.

'Elsie and Tillie and Lacey' kept up their whining and for the first time, I noticed the Malay amah, that Mother Paul had forgotten to introduce into my line of refugees. Maybe Mother Paul was a snob, as most nuns are, but I think it was because Raihana was so unobtrusive, so very camouflaged, that nobody ever took any notice of her, least of all her three charges.

"I think that the three little princesses may cry out and the bad men know we are here. I have fear that I cannot keep them from crying for help and if they do, we will all die surely."

"I'll see to it," Suzy said smartly. "I have good experience of being the amah of a spoilt little white mem."

There was small laughter in her voice and I was thankful that she had not been snuffed out like a candle for ever. I stood at the side of the handcart and listened to her address to the oil princesses. Then we crouched in the straw like all the others and I hid my ears against the shouts and the shooting and the savagery. Of course they came along the trail, like hounds on a breast-high scent. I lifted my head against my own orders and saw the honourable white habits, blood-stained, worn for comedy now . . . saw the cross they carted along for mockery . . . saw Mother Paul's own rosary with the heavy silver crucifix worn round the peaked hat of one of the guerillas and knew that she must have parted with her life first.

They had loaded the harmonium on a farm cart and were pulling the shafts themselves.

We let them past and they searched the house, but never thought to look in the straw shed and I lay silent and prayed to Fred to see to revenge for me, for I was unorthodox in my prayers and I knew myself very tired and very useless. I had more faith in Fred. Three of them were trying to play the harmonium and not able to make much music — only much laughter and then they were gone.

Gordonstoun lit a small fire after a while. We cooked rice and fish and ate it with our hands. We lay on blankets on the floor of the house and got the children settled.

Suzy and I sorted the medical kit they had given us and saw how much we had of everything, and how very little it was, and we lay down and I slept like the dead and woke in the first light, in sudden terror.

They had come back, the little men. I had not thought it possible and I knew myself as no leader. Then I heard Suzy laugh and still the awful noise went on outside the house. The Hopper had wakened and transformed to delight. He ran down the veranda steps into the yard.

"A donkey," he shouted. "A donkey."

Sure enough there was a donkey in the yard and the Grasshopper stroking its velvet nose and God only knew where it had come from! It was just the jetsam of war, as we were ourselves and very hungry. There were potatoes in a clamp in the earth of the yard. The donkey had nosed them out and was helping herself, so that first morning we had rice and fish again and potatoes baked in their jackets in the ashes, and we went on our way and Jenny rode on the donkey's back and after that the 'Little Hopper' called her 'Mary'.

How could we be happy, but we were for the most part. We knew the nuns must be dead. We knew that we were in danger, and the day was a typical tropic day, as if we lived and breathed in a steam bath of sweat. We must not travel by day, so we stayed hidden and we tried to play some children's games, but the Arab girls thought them foolish.

I kept an eye on Jenny and presently I examined her and thought she was near enough to her time.

We had a committee meeting and decided to call the donkey 'Fanny' — but the little boy still called Jenny, Mary.

Thereafter I built up a series of waking-sleeping dreams of every malpresentation and abnormality, that could occur in midwifery and Suzy was too busy with the treacle triplets to notice my anxiety. Had she not been an amah to myself? I was thinking of the safety of the Rotunda and how all one had to do was to send back a chit to the porter and the Flying Squad would arrive, but Suzy was laughing in my ear.

"These three have been born to privilege and that has twisted their view of life and pinned a million dollar ransom on their three little bottoms. I think I smack it out of them. They must learn that in the awful new state, privilege is gone."

She was getting better from that first awful silent grief. It was I, who imagined myself falling short of courage . . . and so we went on. We missed two days march because one of the Arab children was ill with gastro-enteritis. I gave her some of the medicine the nuns had packed for us and read the label. '*Mist, Kaolin pro Infant.*' I knew about the copious fluids, and that meant well water boiled in the black pot, that cooked all our meals. One hour, she seemed to be at the door of death and the next she was better and that night we moved on, but our pace was slow, and we had no compass and we walked in circles again. We were indeed a straggling little army and morale was low, because of heat and the discomfort and the danger and I knew myself inadequate to keep spirits high.

Then there was the day, we caught fresh fish and boiled it, and although it tasted of cotton wool and pins, we relished it and I doled out a pill of 'Vitaminorum' to everybody and some anti-malarial stuff and wished that I had paid more attention to tropical medicine.

The track was rough and our footwear was sketchy and there were sores that blistered first and then festered and ran septic. Day passed day, slowly and always in the back of my mind was the nightmare of the girl, now riding on Fanny, the donkey, and regarded by the 'Little Hopper' as 'Mary, Queen of Heaven', on her way to Bethlehem.

He tilted his head to get me in the focus of the big lenses on his nose.

"I know it's not true, Doctor, but it's a happy thought . . . and God would look after Jesus in the stable and you will look after Jenny, for you are a doctor and all doctors are kind."

Once or twice, we came on a village, which took us in and treated us with what hospitality it could offer, but I was uneasy that a runner might go on ahead of us and take twenty pieces of silver to betray us.

One night, as we started on our way in the middle of a plain of rice fields that spread for miles, with no sign of human habitation a big dog came out of the darkness and made much of us, though he shrank from our outstretched hands and it was obvious he had been ill-treated. If he had appeared at Cruft's, he might have been an Irish Wolfhound. As it was, he attached himself to us and slept close against Gordonstoun's side and thereafter was his creature. We had called the donkey, Fanny. We called the dog, 'Dog' and he came to the call and caught animals for us to eat and if they were not to our taste, he was glad of them himself and so we went along. It was mainly through rice paddy fields and we could see where work might be done, when the rains came, but for now, the people seemed to have been garnered themselves and divided out into labour camps, maybe cooperatives and I wondered uneasily if we were back in Cambodia. At night, in the darkness, we passed silently by and Suzy had changed the three little girls out of all recognition. Now they played 'I spy with my little eye, something beginning with . . . ' They played 'The farmer wants a wife'. They even invented games of their own, and perhaps they were happier than any of us. Their father was a mighty man. Soon he would come for them and chop men's heads off for the way they had been treated, but they had a hard look they reserved for Suzy.

On the thirteenth morning we found the well and I was too thirsty to care about sterility. I drank deep from it and knew that I was foolish, for I made the others wait to drink cooled boiled water. The next day I was ill with fever and there is no future in self diagnosis. I kept the news to myself and that night we went on the march and I watched the stars in the sky and wondered why they wheeled sometimes and refused to stay in one place for long enough to keep my bearings. I knew that I had not fulfilled the mission, that Mother Paul had given me. I had comforted Suzy because Fred was gone. I had talked about him with praise. I had no idea in the world what I could do, if Jenny's baby went wrong. As it was, I said that everything was fine, but it was one of those presentations that might be breech or vertex. '*Breech with extended legs*', I told myself and wanted another opinion and Suzy smiled at me and said it would be as easy as shelling peas and then I started in to wonder what I would do if Jenny had no milk and we travelled all through the tropic night and I had a pain in my stomach, that bent me double and there was no future in depressing the others. I had an

idea that we were still in border country
. . . and I was ill. I pretended to eat my
rice, but I was sick of rice and so were
we all and no salt to go with anything.
I imagined that there might have been
a dead animal at the bottom of the
well and I walked at the head of the
procession, as I always did and Jenny
on the donkey at my side and for some
reason that night, Dog stuck as close to
me as he could get, licked my hand.
When I sat down to rest, he sat tight
against me and shivered, as if he knew
I was afraid.

Then I was back at the head of
the procession again, my hand between
Fanny's ears to scratch her, my fingers
running down along her hogged mane to
rest at the cross of her withers.

I was surprised to find that Jenny was
leaning forward to speak to me.

"Doctor Stuart, I don't want to bother
you, but I think the baby's started. I
had the first pains before we set out
tonight. There's no worry and maybe
it's nothing, but I've had a show. The
pains are harder."

I will never forget that moment, if I

live to be an old old woman. The day was coming up and now we might rest. We were at the top of a small rise, with the sun breaking the rim of the horizon, for the heat of the tropics to come blazing down . . . and no rain yet, not for a long time yet. The whole plain stretched out in front of us in gold and amber and brown and there was an upturned boat and one oar, thrown down beside it and fisherman's nets and a round straw hat. Dog's head was heavy in my hand as I looked up and smiled at Jenny.

"We'll make camp. Not to worry! Everything will be fine. It's not every day we have a baby."

I thought of Grandfather in Glenmore and how worried he must be. I thought of Grant in Kuala Lumpur and willed him to come to our help. "Grant! Grant! Grant!" I prayed.

I had started out in black slacks, but they were shorn to the knee by now. I had cut my shirt sleeves short too and my shirt was in rags. My sandals were flapping against my feet and I had cropped my hair short. There was no black velvet ribbon in it. It curled all over my head and nowhere was there any piece longer than three inches. My face was dirty after the night's march and the sweat was sticking the cotton of my clothes to my skin and I was tired, tired, tired . . . dead . . . dead . . . dead . . . dead . . . tired . . .

There was camp to strike and a place to find to hide through the day. There was Jenny in labour and there were instruments to boil and a child to deliver through long hours. There was a mother to be alive and a baby to be alive and Jenny only a baby herself, a little probationer nurse.

Maybe he thought at first, that I was a boy. I must have looked like enough to a boy, with the short hair and the cut off slacks and the slight hungry body. I knew him at once, for he had not changed, only grown as tough as any commando. There was the roar of a jeep, as it made nothing of the rise. It was upon us before we had time to take cover and I thought that this was the end for us all. I met his eyes bravely and I expected the coarse negroid features of the little men. The camouflaged battle-dress was a change from the black, but they were all the same. Then I saw the fair hair and the sun-tanned face, the eyes as green as the seas off Scarba on a sunny day. It was a happy dream. There was no reality in it. I was in some delirium, yet it was the same voice, I remembered, and I might have been leaning against the sea wall at Glenmore again, watching the speed bird take the bay in a curve.

"Hello there Holy family! Are you really there or are you some sort of a mirage — but is there the remotest possibility that I'm addressing Dr Virginia Stuart? If I told you the job I've had meeting your plane at Kuala Lumpur, you'd never believe me!"

6

Interlude

I LIFTED my hand from the cross on the donkey's back and I walked up the steep of the rise towards the jeep, saw him step over the side, his straw hat tilted over his eyes and still a bright ribbon on it. He took it off to greet me and then threw it back into the jeep and grabbed both my shoulders between his hands.

"You're ill," he said. "You're out on your feet. Don't they know you're ill?"

"Jenny's started to have her baby. We got to the Convent and the nuns gave us a mission. They had a hospital, but they tried to . . . they were all shot down and we had this job to do."

The thoughts were all mixed up in my head and I knew what I was saying but could get no sense into it and I tried to remember where I had seen him in a straw hat with a ribbon on it, tilted over maybe the back of his head or maybe over his eyes.

"I've been to Mother Paul's," he muttered through his teeth. "You can't tell me anything I don't know."

He was holding me against his chest and I thought how tough he was and knew that he did not give a damn for man nor beast. I had a feeling as if I could put down all my troubles at his feet, he would pick them up.

"Mother Paul was a friend of mine," he said and his voice rumbled through his chest to my ear. "An old friend from way back. I know what went on there — don't distress yourself with it now. I paid her debts for her. That's what's taken me so long to come up with you. God blast it! Maybe I'd have let them get away with it, if they hadn't thought to thieve that old harmonium. They won't steal any more . . . not anything from anybody — ever."

His eyes went over my head to the small group gathered in front of us by now. He remembered where he was and his voice was full of joy all at once and no sound of the spilling of blood in it.

"Hello there, Menzies," he said, and he pronounced it 'Mingiss' in the Scots way and I was glad of it and it lifted my heart back to Glenmore in some magic carpet way. "It's glad I am to see your father's son and to know we have your hand in this Exodus to the Promised Land. Isn't it a pity they haven't set Gordounstoun here in the tropics? We might have been glad of all those cold baths at dawn of day?"

It was impossible that there was laughter. Even the three little princesses were laughing, for he asked them if they could sleep on seven mattresses of goose down and know if there was a single pea under the lot and soon he might get word to their father that they were safe.

He held my hand in his and he led me back to Jenny and scratched Fanny between the ears and then ran each ear through his fingers and told Jenny there was no cause for alarm. Hadn't she a doctor and a nurse, but there wasn't much time to spare. He gathered the whole situation into his hands, as Montgomery might have done in the war days, in the war that is past and done, and done . . . done . . . He took Suzy into his arms, as he had done myself and he whispered into her ear and she caught that bright quality he had. She was away in the twinkling of an eye and rummaging about in the hand cart, to find the dressings — stowing them in the jeep, helping Jenny down from the donkey and into the vehicle. Then he had the 'Little Hopper' by the front of the shirt and the small boy with his head back and the enormous spectacles, throwing out the sun, and Grant had Gordounston by the shoulder now.

"We'll go on ahead in the jeep. There's a house up the track. I'll draw you a plan . . . " His toe etched out a line and another line that turned off and a cross that marked something and the squiggle that meant a stream. The medical stuff was all loaded.

"Sorry to leave you and you'll not move till tonight. You have food and you have water and you have bamboo camouflage. I will see thee at Philippi, Gordounstoun."

I was standing beside him at the jeep

and Suzy was in it and Raihana, the Malayan amah.

"Maybe the Sheik thought she was two a penny, but she's a pearl without price in this situation," Grant said to himself and then I think he said it was time to get the doctor sober, but I've never been quite sure of it, for there he was scratching about in his haversack and turning stuff over in the jeep with a haste, that had not been in him before. Then he was back beside me again and I was in the front seat of the jeep and he had a phial of some medicine in his hand, that he wanted me to drink. I took it from him and there was no label to it. It was black and smelt foul.

"I got it from the Snake Temple in Penang," he told me and dared me not to be amused, I, who thought I played tragedy. I shook my head. I was a qualified medical practitioner and I knew that one must never use unlabelled bottles of medicine.

"I'll be well enough in an hour or two," I croaked and he told me shortly that there was not an hour or two left.

"If you don't drink it, I'll force it down

your throat as if you were a beast," he said and he saw I was scared of him and he turned to coaxing me and said there was no harm in the stuff. It had even cured Rat Fergusson, when he had one foot in the grave, and who was I to know what he was talking about! Then he had me in the crook of his arm and the bottle against my lips and there was no turning my head away and it tasted of every filth in the world and smelt up into my nostrils and I thought of 90 per cent proof, and I remembered the mountain dew from the stillie in the Scots hills. I might have swallowed liquid fire, for the way it burnt me down to the sandals. I took a deep breath of the flames from hell. When I exhaled, I was surprised that fire did not emerge from my mouth, like a dragon's breath — and his arm about me still.

"You're a braw bonnie lassie," he said against my ear, his voice all Scots. "You've had ower much to bear, but you've carried it fine — and I'll carry it for a wee bittie now, but I'll tell ye, in case there's no time left to us, that I'll love you till the day I die and beyond that, down eternity. There's times I ask myself when I took such a fancy for loving you and I think it was at the sea wall at Glenmore, or maybe at the Scots airport that first day . . . but when I saw you today, I knew it was you and me till the end of creation."

Maybe he had not said it. Maybe I imagined he said it, for I was really ill, or so it seemed . . . no use at the head of a crusade. He started the jeep and we bumped along the trail and I thought we came to a small track that branched off to the right, but I was back in Glenmore half the time, feeling the wind coming in from the Isles to chatter my teeth. I felt deadly sick. I was going to be sick and disgrace myself, but he told me shortly that it was all right, we were almost there. I imagined that we were coming into a forest for the sun cut off. There was a fine house with a reed roof, a house that stood on stilts, as they all seemed to do, against the rainy season and then this would be flooded and it might be a great sea of water and the fish would breed and be caught for food and for selling. There was a river they dammed up and it was time to get out of the jeep and Jenny was white with pain.

I was conscious of somebody holding my head while I got sick. There was no shame to it, for it was a person who loved me. How else could he not feel revulsion at my heaving sides, but his voice was kind. There was a bucket of cold water and he apologised before he emptied it over me. Then he took a clean linen handkerchief and wiped my face, told me he missed the black velvet bow in my hair.

I was my own man again. It was impossible. Perhaps I was shaky about the knees, but I was able to help lay a blanket on the floor of the house. I was able to get the instruments set out on a boiled piece of lint and I was ready to stand, with a mask across my face and prepare to deliver a baby.

I could see Suzy across from me and the Malay girl boiling water. I could see Grant watching us from the other side of the room. We were coming to the finish and no ease from the pain, but pain could not last for ever.

"It's good to hear a baby cry," I said

for no reason in the world. "It's when a baby is silent, that I worry."

I smiled at Jenny and knew that a smile was just a crinkling of the mask, that had been in the pack, they had given us at the mission — and Grant said he had paid Mother Paul's debt and that must mean he had killed them, but that was a thought for another day. I went through the perfect motions of being a doctor, well skilled in obstetrics.

"Soon over now, Jenny. Each pain is one you won't have again and the baby in your arms and its father's death not a death, but a passing of life to life . . . "

It was coming down fast and there was no cause for all the torture of worry I had suffered. It slipped out into my hands, like a little wet fish. It opened its small mouth to cry — and here was no Rotunda Hospital, only the same sound.

"La, la, la, la, la, la."

I said it was a son and Jenny reached out her arms for it. The cord was severed. It was the same glory of childbirth at Christmas, even if it was here in this awful place.

I thanked God in my heart, as was my custom at such times. Here was a Wednesday's child indeed, which might have far to go. Grant had got the three-bladed fan to work. It connected with a windmill outside and usually it worked. We put Jenny in the coolest place in the room, right under the fan and she went asleep.

The night was coming on and we must keep a look out. Grant spread blankets by the window and he and I must take turns to watch the road. I went asleep, while he took first shift and of course, he did not wake me. It was dawn, when I started up and before I could stop myself I asked him if he had meant all the things he had said to me. I could see his face in the light of a dying moon and there was no carelessness about him now.

"I said them and I meant them."

"About the day at the sea wall, or maybe at the airport and you with the long scarf," I pursued.

"Aye."

I did not seem to care any more that there was only a small chance that either of us ever came out of this alive. I knew I loved him and that death cannot conquer love. There was a great surge of joy and I turned to him. Then we saw them coming up the track and he was laughing and telling me that one day, I might be the Mistress of Slievenailra Castle, so he had better tell me that the medicine he had given me to drink had not been from the Snake Temple in Penang.

"It was stuff I got in Johnny's Bar in Bangkok for a cure for Rat Fergusson's hangovers — never let me down and I hope it still does to him what it did to you. We're going to need Rat Fergusson. My God! How we're going to need him ... "

The sun was coming up and first came Dog, reaching the verandah in one leap to jump all over us, going over to sniff at the baby. Now the children were crowding in, forgetting all tiredness and here was the stable scene all over again with the clean smell of the rice straw, and today was another day.

We rested for a week at the stilt house and if he was master of Slievenailra, here he was master too. He was man to man with Gordonstoun. He treated 'the Little

Hopper' with respect. He elevated the boy to be Chief Watch Man, for Frazer, as his proper name was, could climb like a monkey. For all the tilted head and the big lenses, he could spy a stranger at six miles away, so a camouflaged platform was made in the highest tree and the boy was faithful to his post.

We planned drill for emergency and one day, we needed it. They came in the same black battledress and they turned over the house, but they found nothing. We lay hidden in a thick clumo of brushwood, Jenny with the baby suckled at her empty breast, the jeep under a pile of rice straw. They had been seen from far off by Frazer and thereafter we called him our 'Safe-keeper'.

We were well off the beaten track, but still on the border. Few people came past and they wanted no part of us. They had all the trappings of flight, goods piled on a handcart, a mule perhaps, or hens in a crate, the rice, always the rice. Once we gave them some potatoes and they grabbed them and scurried away with no backward look at us, no word of thanks.

Grant took notice of every detail. The tin of Nestle's milk had run out and Jenny could not feed the baby.

"I have a journey to do, maybe two days, but more likely less. I haven't much petrol left. I've got to get some signals on their way."

He took my shoulders in his hands and said he would try to get a word to Scotland to my grandfather. He knew I was worried about Glenmore. Then he saw my face and changed the subject quickly.

He gathered the three little girls in his arms and told them the story of Beauty and the Beast and they giggled and said that Beauty was a silly girl to ask for a rose. She should have asked for emeralds and diamonds. He swung away from them and spoke to Jenny . . . told her that the place was full of baby-food. He promised to bring some back. In the meantime, there were three coconuts for milk.

Then the jeep was gone in a spurt of the stony pebbled ground and the place was lonely without him. Suzy was silent and worked too hard in the hot sun.

Raihana was tormented by her three charges, who never stopped asking her when the Tuan was coming back. Little Hopper stayed up in the crow's nest all day to watch for the jeep's return. Gordonstoun made an inventory of all the stores, chopped wood for the fire, dug potatoes and with Dog at his heels went out to catch dinner.

We spent a wretched night and then in the morning, the Little Hopper nearly fell down the tree in his haste to tell us that Slievenailra was on the way home.

"I saw the ribbon on his hat and he has somebody with him, an old gentleman in the back with a white beard."

He drove into the road and jumped out to greet us. There had been a face over his shoulder true enough, but it was a nanny goat and it jumped out of the jeep after him and trotted at his heels, a brown animal with witch's eyes and a white beard, that matched her white chest and legs.

"There's all the milk you could possibly want," he said, "And I didn't steal it. I saw her the other day a few miles back, just before I came on your party. Her people have cleared off and left her, so she's an outcast. I think she likes me."

We were high with gladness that he was safe and we all laughed about what the Little Hopper had said about the old man with the white beard, but Grant kissed my cheek and took the boy off to help him cover the jeep in camouflage with rice straw and well we all knew that the nanny goat would make the difference between life and death to Jenny's baby, just as surely as Grant made the difference to every one of us in the stilt house between happiness and sorrow and maybe fear.

If I close my eyes now, I can see again the room with the three-bladed fan whirling over our heads. It bestowed cool air on us like a blessing. Jenny was propped on her blanket on the floor and the baby enjoying goat's milk. Raihana had gathered the three little girls together round her like chicks about a hen. Grant was sitting on a log of wood, that Gordonstoun had brought in for a seat for him, lecturing us that it was time we stopped calling the boy by that foolish name. "His name is

Menzies. Maybe you're all too ignorant to put the right sound on it, but to us Scots, it's 'Mingiss'." His eyes gathered in the Scots contingent, the Little Hopper — Menzies and maybe myself, and great favour to me. He drew me to sit on the floor at his knee and his arm, as if unintentionally about my shoulder, and it had the same fire in it to my senses as Rat Fergusson's draught had had that first day. The children were clambering for a story and he must have been very tired. I opened my mouth to start off on some of the old well-used children's tales, but his fingers caressed my shoulder and I knew he spoke to me alone.

"Maybe it's time I was telling you what it's like at Slievenailra on the isle of Turnish. Some of us know how it is in the Hebrides, but 'twill be no harm to hear it again." Here a pause till he went on again.

"The best time was at Christmas. We brought in a Yule log and the Christmas tree."

We had a small brazier in the stilt house made of an empty tin and burning wood, for the comfort — against the chill of the night and also to keep the mosquitoes away. The light shone on our faces and perhaps we looked like some Dutch oil painting from hundreds of years ago. There was a timelessness about us, the goat in her stall in the corner, Fanny, the donkey nearby, Dog close against Gordonstoun and his head on the boy's foot.

Suzy had curled herself into a ball and her head was on my lap, her face turned away from the light, her eyes closed, yet gradually his voice called her up from the cruelty of the past.

Yet somehow, I knew and he knew, that he and I were alone and face to face, in some other world in both our minds, and this was his way of paying court to me, of telling me that with a great surety, I, too, would go up the mountain on the day before the Eve of Christmas. If it had been snowing, we'd take a sled to drag the log down the brae, but sometimes it might be easier to get the log and the tree into the burn below the fall, and float them down as lumber-men might. Still — if the frost was hard the fall would be like a diamond chandelier.

"One hundred and fifty feet it is and a glory every day of the year. There are times when the salmon come to spawn, but there's a salmon ladder on the far side a bit, and they can come up from one pool to the next, but that's not Christmas yet, with the mountain all snow and the cattle safe in from the hills, and the sheep in the fold, and horses warm in the stables."

He was spreading his life out at my feet and asking me to accept it and there was humility in him and no grandeur, yet there was a wild fierce pride to him too.

"The Christmas tree must be twenty six feet tall, maybe a wee bittie more or less. There's a gallery and you lean out to put the star on the top branch of all and the eldest son had the right of it . . . while he's a bairn and when he finds a wife, his own son does it and so on. It's an honour, though maybe it's foolish."

He was gone away from me and was thinking of something else and there was a sadness about him and his voice soft.

"Maybe it's the running of the salmon

I liked best. There was such a bravery to them and the way they would never be bested, but went on and on to die at last, but they had propagated their kind and the next year, the salmon would run again and on and on up the years, too. The people used to come to see the salmon ladder, not that there are many folk on Turnish, but it's a bonnie place and I wish we were there this minute."

His fingers ground pain into my shoulder and there was a harsh side to him.

"Here we're as safe as if we were in a boat on the edge of Corrievrechan and the outboard engine gone dead on us. I daresay some of you don't know Corrievrechan, but it's a whirlpool, where the tides between the isles run every way and when the water's high and the wind rises, it makes a witches' cauldron and nobody can come alive out of it."

The Little Hopper was tilting his head to look at Grant and he had the same serious old wisdom he always had and we knew now that his name was Fraser, spelt with an 's' and it was time we stopped making fancy names for honourable Scots folk.

"You can anchor in the centre of Corrievrechan if you have a cable made from virgin's hair," the Little Hopper said, and Grant's look defied us to make fun of the child's words. There was a depth in his eyes and a smile that twisted his lips.

"It's a pity you thought fit to cut your hair," he said to me. "If you were to let it grow again and maybe longer, you would be wearing the black velvet bow again and maybe if you were in the Isles, a man could brush it, till it shone like ice and wind it into a great chain, that would keep a boat safe in the midst of Corrievrechan or any great whirlpool in the whole world and keep himself in chains to you, till the day he died . . . "

My mind goes back to linger on that evening in the Robinson Crusoe settlement in the shade of an enchanted wood. We were just inside the Vietnam border, but across the line lay the newly formed Democratic Kampuchea and Grant had turned his mind off the thoughts of Turnish in the Hebrides and was filling us in on what happened in Cambodia and from the crow's nest in the tree the Little Hopper could have looked to the west and seen its rice fields there.

Grant nodded his head towards the Secret State and said that no doubt some of us would have heard of the big city of Phnom Penh.

"It's empty, completely empty, and a cordon thrown round it to keep it that way. I've been there. I know. It's as if an atom bomb had been dropped. There is dust blowing in the streets, but the entire population has been driven out — driven out to the countryside to live as best they can . . . or to die. Their property has gone to the State. All the cities and the big towns are the same. The people must get out and join a labour camp and work their living in the fields or escape. There is no coinage, no hospital, no doctors, no schools, no shops, no factories. You form into a group of people on a cooperative farm or camp and you work with what tools you have. Here are no bulldozers, no great combine-harvesters. They're trying to dam water, but mostly they pedal it up on a bicycle contraption . . . and men or women or children do it. They dig with shovel and spade. The children work alongside the adults and Cambodia wants a population explosion, so marriage is encouraged, but no ceremony about it, just a permit from the Co-operative and the children will probably be handed over to the government in the years to come. It's history in the making, as it always is, and we're living it. Children are crewing the fishing boats. Kampuchea wants new citizens, and each child is a unit of work. Three crops of rice are to be taken from the paddy fields in each year now and there's a banditry on the border pillaging Vietnam for rice. Hence the gun-fire. Vietnam should be their friend and neighbour, but Vietnam is Enemy Number One. They're at each other's throats and we're set right between them . . . People are getting out of Cambodia in their hundreds, escaping through Vietnam to the sea maybe, escaping across the sea from the Delta — with nothing like reason in their minds, only a lemming feeling that it's time to go."

I closed my mind to anything but the thought of Slievenailra Castle and the ice of the long water-fall and perhaps to the brushing of a skein of white hair, fresh-grown. There were oceans to be crossed and it was easy enough in dreams, but in life, there was as much chance for us as a butterfly winging out over an ocean. Grant and I might do it, get back to Turnish in the Hebrides, but I knew this was a pipe-dream. There was to be no more of it, only this short evening in the house in the forest and the fire in the brazier lighting our faces. This might be all that was to be of a lifetime of complete happiness.

Here was a night for fantasy . . . yet life went slowly on, so slowly, slowly on.

Elsie, Lacie and Tillie told us the Arabian Nights stories of their lives, how happy they had been with African slaves to wait on them, and no wish denied. They had wanted a giant rocking horse from Harrod's and their father was so rich and powerful, that three rocking horses had been flown in, one for each of them, as big as a real pony, but they liked best the three green singing finches, who had sung their hearts out. They had voices like the serin bird, that people called the canary and they had a gold cage, specially made, but still they broke their hearts for their own land, poor pretty little birds!

They had died. One day they had been stiff and dead, with their small claws clenched and their yellow breasts to the sky, but their backs still as green as the grass in an oasis and no singing left.

There was a moral here somewhere and I wondered if the three small princesses were just three small singing grassfinches — caught in the cage of this border country and all the grasslands of their father's money lost to them for ever.

I pushed back the morbid thought and prayed that Grant would get us all out safely. Maybe Rat Fergusson was something of a Scarlet Pimpernel. Maybe he was waiting for us and he would spirit us out secretly. Perhaps Grant and he had some planned escape route, well tried and safe, and I wondered why Grant always seemed cheered at the thought of Rat

Fergusson, but the time for bed had come and next evening, Grant was setting out again on some mission of his own, for there was something he wanted to misappropriate.

That afternoon, he had lined us all up in the shade of the verandah and he had picked up a bamboo cane in the yard and had it tucked under his arm, an officer on parade. He made a game of it, but I knew it was no game, but something of mighty importance.

There we stood in a raggety line and he walked along in front of us like the sergeant major of drill in the Argyll and Sutherlands and took in every detail. He stopped opposite the three Arab children and picked Suzy up in his glance, tapped the cane on their heads and told her that hair must come off.

"These three are to have a short back and sides, Sister, and you'll do it. Virginia will hold them if needs must, but they must be shorn. See to it."

He looked at Gordonstoun and said he was man-sized and at the Little Hopper, he paused and set the spectacles straight on the snub nose.

"Later on, I'll take those glasses for safe keeping, Fraser. Just for now, as soon as I leave, get to your post on look out. Get them into cover, Menzies, if he spies soldiers. Ignore the stragglers to the north, going west to east. There may be quite a few of them, but they're after their own business, not ours . . . and as for size, Fraser, I'd say boy's size, but one day you'll be a fine man like your father, and your father will have as much pride in you as I have."

He paused opposite me and told me he knew me well, but that my hair must stay short, but only till we came safe home. He dismissed us then and our spirits were raised, but he put his hand in my arm and drew me aside.

"I think I got a message out to Glenmore — almost surely your Grandfather will know . . . We're almost ready. When we go, we swim against the current. They're getting out of Cambodia like Lemmings. They're running into Vietnam and they're getting gunned down, some of them. I plan to go the other way. Nobody in their right senses would try the west escape route. That way lie the labour camps and they're controlled. We'll just have to hitch a ride. Rat Fergusson is our hope. He'll wait as long as he dare, that is, if he hasn't got himself stuck in Johnny's Bar in Bangkok. I wouldn't put it past him, yet I think not."

I asked him if Rat Fergusson was like the Scarlet Pimpernel and he laughed at that.

"Maybe aye, maybe no," but he himself was off an hour before sundown and would be back in the morning.

He put his arm round me and kissed my cheek, before he climbed into the jeep and I wanted to clutch at his shoulders and beg to go with him. Instead I said "Haste ye back", and thought of the sea-wall in Glenmore and wished that I was in Slievenailra Castle in a window looking down on the frozen fall and his hand in my hair.

"I will see thee at Philippi."

He scattered us with pebbles, as he drove off and the hat was tilted on the back of his head. There was need to shade his eyes for he was facing to the west and I knew that any of us with sense of direction was trying to shut out the thought of the route he was travelling. He might tell us that he was a familiar figure. The media of the world knew him and he came and he went and his words were heard across the world. Even the Secret State had to be tactful with him, but I knew that Cambodia had no respect for any law ever made and well I knew that Cambodia was where he was headed, but why he went I had no idea. There was the goat to milk and the baby to feed and the baby slept and that satisfied Jenny, baby and goat. We tried to sleep that night in this house that Jack built — from goat to milk and from milk to baby and from baby to Jenny and from Jenny to me. There must have been such an upsurge of prayer for his safety at the gates of heaven, that he came back before dawn.

We heard the engine in the night and rushed to our hiding places and a jeep drove into the centre of the yard and in the half light, we saw the hat still tipped over the back of his head, just as it had been and himself lifting his leg over the driver's door.

"It's all clear. You can come out of

cover. Mission accomplished. There's a column on its way . . . "

We crept out and gathered about him, but he had not spent all his time in the jeep. There was a gash in his shirt and he had travelled part the way on his stomach. His face was dirty and he had made a sketchy effort to clean up that had left him like an unwashed school boy. I fetched him a bowl of water and a towel and he muttered something about Sherlock Holmes and remarked that I was more School Ma'am than Doctor.

I countered that by asking him what he would like for breakfast and he looked round at the circle of our faces.

"A plate of porridge and salt not sugar and two fried eggs and buttered toast, and fresh-baked Scots baps and tea, that you could trot a mouse on."

Even Suzy was laughing with us as she served the salt fish in milk and told him it was genuine Finnan haddock. Then we had rice cooked in milk too and finally pancakes made from flour and milk and we all thought it the best breakfast ever, because he was back safe again.

Then he gathered us on the verandah

and he went to the jeep and collected a bundle from the back of it, threw it down on the floor and three peaked caps escaped from it and brought our merry mood to a halt. He cut the string with a pen-knife and I saw that he had acquired black cotton clothing, coats and trousers, of various sizes and a heap of thonged sandals, head scarves, straw hats.

"I had only to find a military stores. They issue stuff once a year to every member of a co-operative labour camp, or they intend to." He saw that the three little princesses were shy about their shorn heads and he lifted them up and kissed them in turn, perched a sun-hat on the crew cuts and told them they were setting a new fashion for Paris. Goodness knows it had been murder for Suzy and me to achieve the hair cut and Jenny had been in hysterics with laughter and the Malayan amah Raihana, in floods of tears, and now the three children were delighted.

"I must sleep for a while. I want you all to get kitted out. I think the clothes will fit near enough. God knows about the sandals! Sort them out, I'm for a rest now. I'll review the troops at tea-time."

He took a blanket and lay down in a shaded place under a tree and was asleep between one second and the next.

Gordonstoun had put the jeep back under its heavy cover of straw, had piled the straw high. The Little Hopper was faithful in his tree house and the rest of us sorted the garments.

Then we were on parade again in the zephyr from the three-bladed fan and Grant clad in black cotton trousers and shirt and a cotton scarf on his head, pirate fashion, thonged sandals on bare feet, his face dirty, his feet dusty. We lined up before him in our black outfits and he walked down the rank. We were too clean. Had we not understood his plan? We had been walking for days. In half an hour, he had transformed us into an unhappy group, who had been dispossessed, who had lost home and present and maybe future too.

"If you must speak, speak French or Malayan. I'm not too sure about Chinese now. Any Indonesian tongue may get by. Best if you keep your mouths shut and if one of us runs into trouble, the others must create a diversion."

He smiled at Raihana.

"As to your three little lassies, if they keep up that whining complaint, they have made so far non-stop, that's O.K. It's international."

He told us his plans. The Little Hopper was to keep watch for one of the labour camp marches. That meant a long slow column of miserable people, with few guards. He planned to insinuate us into it. We would go in two or three at a time from cover by the main road. We would rejoin in the column and so we would proceed.

"We move with the next suitable column. It's on its way. I'll plant you along the route. These columns are all raggle taggle. They carry what personal possessions they can manage. They have goats and donkeys and mules. They have buffalo carts and ducks and hens. There's no order to them. They move ten miles or less in one day. You're to hold yourselves ready. When we get the signal, we move to the culvert under the bridge on the main track, go on from there. We have no more use for the jeep, so we'll let it stay hidden here. It would only draw attention and there's no petrol anywhere."

He put back his head and laughed at our anxious faces.

"This is going to be an awfully big adventure," he said.

Barrie had used the same words. I remembered a theatre in Kuala Lumpur and I must have been very young at the time and home from Scotland for the holidays. We had gone to see a pantomime and Peter Pan was on stage.

"To die would be an awfully big adventure," Peter Pan had said and now I felt a cold wind through my heart, for I knew we were in the midst of an awfully big adventure indeed.

7

"The Awfully Big Adventure"

WE packed our belongings that evening and settled down for the night. Grant and I lay by the window as usual and my hand in his. On the edge of dawning, he spoke to me. I had such a longing for him that he had only to stretch out his arms to me to possess me and he knew it. He told me how it was going to be, this honourable young man.

The day we were wed, he would wait for me at the steps of the altar in the greystone kirk. I would come up the aisle on my grandfather's arm and the piper of Slievenailra would be striking glory from the walls with the skirling of the pipes. The congregation would represent the Isles and the church would be thronged to the door, aye, and outside too. I'd have the Ring of the Eagle waiting to go on my finger, a ring that had come down the generations.

"It's in safe keeping this minute in Edinburgh waiting for myself to put it on your finger."

He turned his face away from me and wished that he might fly away with me on a secret honeymoon and have done with all ceremony and then he laughed in that sudden carefree way he had.

"It might likely kill the old gentleman in Glenmore if we did such a thing. I promise you faithfully, that you'll be there and I'll be there and everything else will fade into a dream."

I leaned myself towards him and almost he took me into his arms. There was no power on earth could stop us, only the shrill calling from the look-out post on the tree and the Little Hopper, racing up the steps of the verandah.

"I can see them. They must have started well before dawn a long column like a snake, winding a mile along the road. They have hundreds of people walking slowly and animals and carts like you said . . . only a few men with rifles, one up front and one at the back and maybe two more — and the people are in black suits, the same as us."

Our house was indeed full of black-suited people but we were well drilled.

"Let's go," Grant said. His hand touched the Little Hopper, collected the spectacles and put them in his own pocket.

"Well done, Fraser. I'll keep these for safety. Now let's get on. We've not over much time."

There was a bridge four hundred yards east of the house. I could hear Raihana cautioning her charges, as we crouched under the culvert.

"You are not to speak — not one word. If you do, men will come with long knives and kill you. Now, there must be no sound."

Then Grant was beside me, almost unrecognisable in the cotton scarf that hid his hair. I had just such a scarf to cover the give-away white. There was nothing about any one of us — but squalor and misery and the dust of a long treck.

"Suzy, Virginia, get ready to go. I'll put the others in along the way. We'll move back to meet up with you by evening. Try to edge forward. Mind how you go . . . I will see thee at Philippi."

He was gone. They were all gone, or most of them. From the other direction, we could hear the sound of voices and cries and animal noises and shouting. They passed over our heads where we hid in the culvert, Suzy and I. Grant had left the goat with us. I had taken one look at the column and it was just as they had described, a shifting of population from one place to another and no military formation to it. People were falling out and rejoining it all the time and nobody cared any more. A woman stopped as they passed over the bridge and came into hiding to relieve herself and did not even look at us. When she rejoined, we went with her, came in beside an ancient Chinese man, who moved over to make room and looked at us . . . with dead eyes.

Throughout the day, we picked up news from the grapevine, that existed even in this miserable place. Suzy started by speaking Chinese to the old man and he told us that every 'unit' got a ration of rice a day and we drank from any good well we passed. It was better not to eat what food we had. Soon there might not be ration rice left and then we could barter with people, who had no rice nor fish.

I saw Jenny ahead of us on the donkey and the baby in her arms. We moved unobtrusively up to join her and there was Gordonstoun with Dog at his heels. There was a kind of many-languaged conversation and we infiltrated forwards, for here was a polyglot society, with bad news being rumoured around, like the dust we shuffled under our feet.

When the sun was lower, they brought rice in aluminium containers and ladled out a small cupful each and by that time, we had thought to get empty baked bean tins. We spoke to people in a patois of French, in English, in Tamil, in Malayan, in Chinese. We collected the news like scavengers and passed it among ourselves and thank God, we were all together now, about two thirds way up the line, towards the front.

There was some bartering. You could change goat's milk into rice or salt. You could change a gold bracelet for a live hen. Little Hopper had acquired a white duck, which he carried under his arm, because it had followed him but there was no chance of it ever being slaughtered for food, for he was determined 'to save its life'.

Little Hopper was a small cheerfulness with a duck instead of his glasses, but the news was bad. We were in Cambodia, but it was no different in Vietnam now. The end of the world had come there too. People had taken to the hills and the forests to escape, mostly those in high office. They were running like mice with no place to hide and they died on the way. They disappeared on the way. Maybe they were murdered.. Australia was far away. They might think to reach Thailand or Malaya . . .

There were labour camps now in Vietnam too. You caught the news in the air, as if you looked at a neon sign and read. It was all the same. They wanted workers on the land. There was no coinage now, no banks or shops, no priests, no temples. The books had been burnt, all the books from the National Library. The ration for every man, woman and child was 300 grammes a day of rice . . . no meat, no salt, fish, no vegetables, no sugar. Every person had registered for a camp for organised labour. We were on our way to one now and it was near the Mekong River. If you refused to work, you starved and this was Cambodia but there was no escape to Vietnam now either. It was from one cooking pot into another.

We were in the column for a labour camp and we had no papers of registration, but Grant reassured me.

"We'll be out of the march before we get there. We're on the right route, for Phnom Penh . . . "

The news came over as if on a ticker tape, only in whispered conversation with strangers.

China was on the brink of a war with South Vietnam. Cambodia and Vietnam were bonfires, that must go up into a mighty blaze of fire and war.

Suzy was as silent as ever. She lived with her thoughts of Fred and resisted all my efforts to talk about him. She wanted no intrusion, yet intrude I did and talked of the old days and laughed about memories, when I wanted to cry. I tried to make him live in our conversation again and remember the happiness, but happiness was gone for her. Then I got the idea of drawing her back into the strangest Snake Temple of them all. God knows there was no scarcity of patients! We dressed wounds. We gave out any drugs we could spare, but best of all, we delivered a baby, poor little creature on its way to Phnom Penh or thereabouts to a labour camp. Suzy held the slippery 'fishy' up between her hands and her face was lit again. I believe that small child saved her soul. She looked after it every day and she began to smile again. She smiled a little bit more every day and she moved up and down the column and was known as 'Sister'. She knew we were making for the labour camp, just south of Phnom Penh, but it was a ghost city, she told me. It was totally empty, for the people had been driven out. It had been a garden city, but now it was guarded by a handful of custodians and its people were gone. There was just this small maintenance population. Our labour camp was a few miles south of the city.

Grant murmured in my ear.

"Rat Fergusson was supposed to be moored at Phnom Penh and that's a hitch, but hitches are life's blood to Rat. Do you know that there was a day, when he hi-jacked a helicopter and its crew and came and picked me out of a hell hole of a prison in Vietnam, when the war was on. I owe him. Oh. God! I owe him! He runs on alcohol, so many kilometres to the pint and he runs alcohol to Cambodia. I met him first in Johnny's Bar in Bangkok. I've owed him ever since. He's an institution in these parts . . . a natural camouflage, does the round trip from Penang Island off Malaya to Phnom Penh in an old paddle steamer. It's like something you might see on the Mississippi. She's got prestige, that old boat. She's got a paddle astern and she has a shallow draught, which is right for the Mekong."

I loved him the more for the small tired smile. I wanted to take him into my arms and lay his head on my breast, but this was forbidden luxury.

"They close their eyes to the old Queen Victoria and her captain, always have done. He'll find where we are or we'll find him. He'll know that we must realise what's happened in Phnom Penh and he knows the Mekong and the China Seas like the palm of his hand."

Then one day, the white duck took off into the skies and the Little Hopper ran after it out of line. There was a rattle of machine gun fire and the child toppled into a bush. Grant's hand held me fast.

"Do you want to risk the whole plan? We'll go back after him presently."

We went back after half a mile to find a tree we had marked down, Grant and I. There was a small white duck that crept out of a brushy patch and it was impossible to believe that a child's hand came after it and that the Little Hopper was unhurt.

We moved forwards and caught up with the column and if people noticed, they did not speak and the duck's eyes gleamed like black currants in the sun and so we crept on along the miles. Our feet were blistered and wrapped in old pieces of rag. We went on, day after day, shuffling across the plain of dry season rice land, yet there were fertile places, where black-clothed women worked on bicycle contraptions to raise the water to the paddy fields and here we saw the sown rice sprouting green — saw labourers, who dug out irrigation channels. It was not the end of the story yet. I thought of a conversation I had had with the Tunka in Malaya, many years ago. If one could get three crops of rice a year from the paddy fields, it might hold off Armageddon. There was small hope of it in my mind, with my half baked bean tin of rice. It was a different world, Malaya, and here they had set learning at nought and that was a foolish thing. What about the child labour? We had had it in England in the pits and in the cotton factories, but we had survived to the glory turned in Dunkirk. Here children worked beside adults and they crewed the fishing boats, but there was this problem of education. Once shut a child's mind to it — but who was I to be judge and executioner? I was only a doctor, who scuffed my feet in the dry path with Suzy beside me and both of us mourning for sorrow, that could never be undone. They died along the route, old people but young people too, ones, who might have become Alexander Flemings, Michaelangelos. We could do little to help them, the ones who might have discovered the cure to cancer and now lay dead at the edge of a dusty road.

Grant came by night to spread his blanket beside mine, take my hand in his — speak soft things to me, promise me Slievenailra and that I would be queen of it, promised that we would walk the mountains together, promised me our sons and our sons' sons and that they would inherit the earth that was Turnish, promised me he would love no other, but this was neither the time nor the place.

In the day was gossip. Vietnam — Cambodia, there was no way out. It was all the same. Shops and homes and banks and hospitals were for looting and robbing. Owners were driven out into the streets to their death. There were hideous waves of suicide in Vietnam. It was going on now, this very minute, with people, who thought it easier to die than to face the reality, of a cruel world. Two and a half kilos of gold was the price of a passport out of Vietnam. Escapers were being stopped, robbed of their possessions and let go free, but there was no place for them to go. Here then was freedom, in Cambodia and in Vietnam. 'Escape, escape, escape' was on everybody's lips, but there was no escape.

At least, in a march to a labour camp, there was daily rice. Always the hunger prodded them on. The rice fields were golden brown and arid, but the monsoons would come and this land would be a sea. Fish would breed for the catching and rations would be better for the people in the camps. Gossip: gossip: gossip. Clothes would be provided and agricultural tools. A man might start living all over again. The march was near its end. Better this than a war. If China comes down against South Vietnam, Cambodia will not escape.

Then one evening, Grant was by my side, lying beside me, taking my hand in his.

"Phnom Penh is almost in sight, five miles at most to its perimeter. Tomorrow evening, this march will arrive at its destination, so I must be away later on tonight. I've got to contact Fergusson. Then we'll pick you up. You'll be well able to take care of the others."

He gave me detailed instructions and I carried them out to the best of my ability, but he had left the same state of emptiness, that he always left after him and I felt so inadequate. As he had instructed, we lay hidden at the side of the road the next morning and let the winding trail of people move slowly on. We had found another bridge culvert and here we stayed and nobody missed us. There was a tree on the horizon and it seemed an easy march, but we came on marshy places and unexpected obstacles. It was like every short cut, that proves longer than it seems. I thought we would never reach that tree. It cannot have been more than four miles off, but it took us the whole day. It was an hour till sundown, when we got to it and the children wanted to stop, but Suzy and I were harsh with them. We turned west beside the Mekong and trudged up river along the bank, surprised at the size of it and at its yellow colour. It carried silt from its journey across half a continent, riches, that could have been, but they ran to waste at the delta. For two – three miles, we trudged along and now we had craft to watch, for there were plenty of them going downstream, people, who were running away, as we were — fishing boats, sampans, rafts, house boats. None of them had any thought of greeting us or of coming ashore. Here were the refugees in force and at long last, here was the shed, that Grant had described to me. Here was the bamboo jetty and the shed and the fishing nets and still they went by as the night fell, the canoes, the rowing boats, the Chinese junks, the launches, all laden down with refugees.

We camped that night in the shed, that was hung with fishing nets and the quick darkness had come down. Upstream was the capital city and downstream was the Mekong delta and beyond that, the whole world via the China Seas, if fortune smiled, but the Mekong ran back through Vietnam.

The shed was on stilts as every building in that watery place was on stilts. We tethered the animals in the security of cover. There was a small tributary river and the next day, we fished there and let the Little Hopper's duck, which he called 'Donald' swim. We caught fish, cooked and ate them and for the next few days we lived on fresh fish and rice and then Donald started to lay eggs and belied his name, so we added egg to our menu and made very merry about it, but Grant had not come and my anxiety mounted. A duck called Donald might lay eggs, but there was no sight of the Queen Victoria coming down river. I strained my eyes looking upstream, willing Rat Fergusson's stern paddle steamer to come. I imagined every horrific adventure, that might have taken Grant to his grave and there were plenty of such in this land. Rat Fergusson, we would know by the oily rag carried in his back pocket. The Victoria would be a stern paddle steamer in need of paint. Grant's voice still echoed in my ear.

"He'll have me battened down below, if I know him, when we come to the jetty. They all know what cargo he carries, have known it for years. He carries alcohol at reasonable rates, and doesn't give a damn for authority."

Then in my mind his voice came back softly.

"Oh, my darling, if we don't come out of this safely, and it's a chancy business, go to Turnish, if you're the one left — go to the castle, tell them how it happened in an upside-down world. Tell that you're my wife, but there was no priest to marry us. Tell them the time ran out on us. We wished to wed in the kirk. That was how it would have been. You should bear my son and they're to take you in and put down green rushes at your feet. They'll have no wish to steal your heritage from you, no, not in Turnish, if you'll walk away with me now."

It seemed impossible what had happened that night. He had taken my hand in his and led me to a small trickle of water, running down towards the Mekong. He had clasped my hand in his and set me at the other side of the stream.

"I, Gareth take thee, Virginia to be my lawful wedded wife, as long as we both shall live, aye, and beyond that."

Our voices had been whispers and

maybe it had never happened.

"I, Virginia, take thee Gareth Grant, to be my lawful wedded husband, as long as we both shall live, for richer, for poorer, for better, for worse, till death do us part, aye and beyond that."

He had told me that we were wedded by the old laws of Scotland and that nobody could set us asunder.

"I've put into writing what's happened between you and me. I'll send a messenger to my solicitor in Edinburgh — but go to Scotland yourself, if things run agley. I love you so very much."

There was a custom, called hand-fasting in Scotland. His voice had been wistful, full of what might have been . . . a whisper, barely audible.

"Nobody can come between us, for we're wedded now. It can never be undone till the last syllable of recorded time."

Then again, and again, and again.

"Go to Scotland. Tell them how it was, in this place. Tell them how I loved you and how you loved me."

I lay on my blanket in the shed on the banks of the Mekong and asked myself if it was all a dream. How I watched for the paddle steamer, while Raihana turned cards face down on the sandy floor!

"Now, we play Pelmanism, one more time. You pick up a matched pair and they are yours. The more you get, the better the winner . . . "

I tried to join in the game but it required concentration and mine had run out. I was full of thoughts of the old paddle steamer. It had a musical device on board, Grant had told me. How I wanted to see the bow of the Queen Victoria and hear the sound of the gallopers at a fair! There was music somewhere far away, but it was probably in my head after three days waiting in this shed. Rat Fergusson had turned down Grant's inflammable cargo, I thought. Why should I hope for anything else? Why should I call him Grant, when his name on my lips should have been Gareth? I was like Jane Eyre and Mr Rochester. Gareth . . . Gareth . . . Gareth . . . come to me, I willed, and picked up another unmatched pair of cards . . . and knew that there were no matched pairs left . . . not for Suzy and not for me.

The Little Hopper was feeding flakes of fish to Donald and snuggling the bird up against his small thin chest, which resembled a scrubbing board more than ever.

The three little Arab princesses were winning the game hands down and I had stopped watching the river.

I just sat there, pretending to play a child's card game and wondered about all the things, that might have happened, wondered what grandfather McLean in Glenmore was doing and if he had heard of the news from Cambodia and Vietnam . . . heard of a crashed plane and every passenger presumed dead.

My eyes were on the door, when it began to move, inching slowly, slowly and a man sidling round the edge of it. Dirty khaki camouflage battle dress, old tennis shoes, a captain's cap, gold braid and all, but the white top, shop-soiled, three – four days growth of beard on his face, a cigarette in the corner of his mouth and a wry twist to his lips, a gun stuffed into his waist-band and mighty ready to his hand too, the description had been good. There was something about him . . . He came across the shed and touched the first card with the toe of a canvas shoe.

"So here's the Holy Family and I didn't believe him . . . bloody donkey and a babe in the manger, a full house and I called him a liar."

I got to my feet and asked him if Gareth Grant was all right and he nodded his head and said "Sure, baby." Then he saw the anxiety in my face.

"He's stowed aboard round the bend upstream. He's fine, swearing blue murder because I made him stay there."

He went to the window and put two fingers into his mouth and let out a serrated whistle, that might have called a hansom cab from four hundred yards up a Sherlock Holmes street. Then his mind was back on the startled faces and the cards.

"Nothing I like better than a game of poker and guns left at the door," he said and his eyes were on me again.

"You'll be the Lady. It's good that you and he managed to find each other in a shaky world. I reckon at this moment, y'd search the seven seas for a shakier world and a better-matched pair."

He took the cigarette out of his mouth and ground it to extinction under the old tennis shoes and I wondered how long it had been since he had played tennis.

"The Laird says there's a goat and a duck as well as the old Ned but where's your look-out, Lady?"

"Gordonstoun's look-out," I excused myself. "We were watching for a paddle steamer."

There was a sound of music that grew loud and louder and Gordonstoun opened the door and let a blast of the music come in, told us that there was a craft drawing in to the wharf and the whole scene was played to the background of 'When the Saints Come Marching In', and I wondered if I had dreamt up the man and the whole of the last feverish days, hand-fasting and all.

"I came on ahead," he explained. "Better to do a recce. There's too many of these sheds on stilts and some of them not so friendly by half. Now this is a right cosy place, but it takes a bit of working on. I can see his point. There's no choice but to take the whole company, but it will be like a bloody ark. The babby has to have the goat for the milk. The Ned's for transport. Gor sends that the duck lays eggs."

The Little Hopper held the duck more tightly to his bony chest and whispered that the duck's name was Donald and that he usually laid an egg a day and Rat's hand tousled the child's hair and I knew the kindness of him.

"If that's the case, I wouldn't trade him for the Koh-i-noor diamond. He'll eat fish and maybe rice and he'll live on weed from the river, if some savage doesn't shove him into a cooking pot and I'll see to his safety personal. Rest easy, Fraser."

So he had our name's too and doubtless all about us.

He scratched the back of his head and put his cap on again and there was a jaunty tilt to it.

"I like it," he said to nobody in particular. "The more I see of it, the more I like it. What's the virtue in doing a job that's as easy as kiss my . . . "

Here came a pause and the word

'hand' substituted quickly and a sideways glance at me.

"I've always hankered after doing a job that's quite impossible. My Gor! I've found it, with the three little sheikesses, two boys and three young ladies, that are the loveliest a man could wish aboard his craft. I trade between Malaya and the capital city of Cambodia — have done for a long time, copra an' spices an' rice an' the little things that genteel people like to lay their hands on. I'm an honest trader, I am, won't find a more reasonable bloke in the whole of Indonesia."

"Emeralds and amethysts and gold moidores," I murmured and he took a cigarette from his breast pocket, and lit it in cupped hands from a match struck on the seat of his pants.

"You're the one for Slievenailra of the Isles, Lady, and he was right about the hair — a crime to cut it. I could have picked you out of a thousand, with the way he talked about you. I'll be mighty glad to have your menagerie aboard. I never lost a cargo yet, not as long as I have enough petrol to keep my engines running."

He was back to studying the duck and he gave us his considered opinion that it was a great advantage that "it was no drake".

"A drake would be off after the first duck he saw," he said. "It wouldn't lay no eggs neither."

The mention of petrol jogged my hospitality. Was I not a Scot bred and I had in my possession a medicine bottle with four ounces of whisky in it. It had been a gift from the Holy Sisters and it belonged in the medicine chest and was labelled *'For medicinal use only'*.

I found a blue enamelled mug and I up-ended the bottle into it, dipped a similar mug into the water jar for myself.

"Maybe you'd wish a dram before we load up?" I said.

I raised my mug.

"Here's to the success of the Queen Victoria and my heart to you for your courage, Captain Fergusson!"

He took the whisky down in two long swallows, gave a long sigh and sucked his teeth.

"Captain Fergusson," he said softly.

"What a grand thing it is to meet up with a lady!"

Then the darkness was coming down in the swift way it had. In the half dusk, I saw the Queen Victoria for the first time, saw the stern paddle and the red duster flying, and the single funnel amidships and a haze of smoke . . . a bridge forward and high, an upper deck . . . a lower deck, that would run alongside the cabins . . . and a row of ports and a stout sturdy, little ship, that was nothing like what I had pictured her. If this ship had done anything, it had gone mine-sweeping in the forties. It was a brave ship for all its present come-down-in-the-world appearance. It had a shallow draft and that was why it could sail the Mekong and yet face the China Seas. He would wait for good weather and then risk the dash across the ocean. Had not somebody said he did not give a tinker's curse for man nor beast? Had I dreamt it all up in one moment between waking and sleeping? Maybe I possessed a second sight, but I knew in that first minute that here was a gallant ship, that had every right to carry the Red

Duster — a gallant captain that had every right to his gold braid rusty as it was. His schemes had gone awry . . . as Robbie Burns said. Then I saw the gangplank going out and I was away from his side and running. I was caught by another sea-man, as my foot touched the deck. He held me close in his arms.

At the top of the wide gangplank Gareth Grant held me close, did not let me free, till he had dried my tears, but by then we were creating a block to embarkation, for the goat was stepping up the plank with as much dignity as the Queen coming to review the Fleet at Portsmouth. Then the children rushed on and the adults walked behind them, but the donkey would have none of it. She was determined never to trust herself on this mighty water, increasingly mighty, since it had been joined by a branch from the Tonle Sap, at Phnom Penh.

There are things that will stick in my memory for ever and this is one of them, never to be forgotten, till I lie in my grave, yet sorrow blots out a great deal of the past in mercy.

Grant . . . Gareth talked the donkey

aboard. He stroked the long ears but first he turned her stern to the river. Then a hand on either side of the bridle and whispering to her. Step by slow step, he backed her up the plank. Her hooves made a hollow sound, but against that came a stutter in the music and my attention was caught by the machine that made it. It was all chrome and flashing bulbs and after the initial stuttering, it took on a new lease of life because of a prompt kick from Rat. It rolled out 'There's a Long Long Trail a-winding . . . into the Land of my Dreams . . . ' and the donkey was on deck. There was a place for her aft, the neatest stall, one could imagine, bedded with rice straw and with a bowl of cut raw potato, mixed with oatmeal. There was a bucket of fresh water. She was tethered to the stern rail and the goat at her side and we went into the confusion common to all embarkation. We were travelling light, but there were blankets and haversacks and water canteens and all the impedimenta of panic escape. It was strange how we ever settled down.

On the main deck was a long cabin

with a seat that ran either side for the length of it. Here we made our blanket beds. The three little 'sheikesses' were segregated to a small cabin with Raihana. We cast off forrard and we cast off aft. The river took us gently, gently down the lazy current and Rat was on the bridge at the wheel, his cap tilted over his eyes, knowing every inch of the voyage, we proposed to make. There were craft moored along the banks for the night and once, an anxious face peered up at him from a sampan.

"Glad to see you again, Mr Fergusson, sir. Always you bring plenty luck. Now all is O.K. Trouble soon go, for you fix everything good. All go O.K. now. You see. But watch at the Vietnam border. There is much firing of guns and even smallest boat searched."

I was on the bridge beside him and Gareth with me and Rat's face was sombre and the music player had got itself stuck into the Long, Long, Trail and he lost patience with it. He ran lightly down the companionway and gave it another sharp kick and it broke into 'Happy Days are Here again' and he said that was an improvement.

He tilted his cap a little more forward and rejoined us on the bridge, took back the wheel from Gareth.

I opened my mouth to ask him where he got the music maker and he grinned at me and I knew the answer before he gave it to me.

"Johnny's Bar at Bangkok," he told me. "It was past its best." Then he put back his head and laughed and he looked just what he was, the king of the Mekong and the master of his own fate and ours too. He didn't give a tinker's damn, they said, but now I thought they were wrong. He cared very much for mankind and he had always cared and would go on caring, and he tried to put my anxiety to flight.

"Don't be thinking about what that there bloke said about the border. I reckon it's a bit rough, the passage, now that there's open war or thereabouts, but I've got through before and I'll do it again a great many times. There's no harm in me. They know it. There's a show I put on for them. They've come to expect it . . . and the more noise we make and the more lights we show, the easier we get by. I'm going to set a play up and I want cast. Most of the company will lie low, but I'll want a few principles. Yourself and Suzy could do it. You're accomplished actresses, must be in the medical line. I've thought of casting you as 'a pair of hookers' and that don't mean we'll catch fish . . . and the laird won't agree, if it comes to that. We'll get by one way or the other. It all depends on the swiftness of the hand deceiving the eye. Maybe it might work. I trade in a very powerful cargo, very explosive too, but maybe it rots men's brains. It gives them courage. I do know that. It's like them small tranquilliser tablets that all the ladies of the west live on."

It was very quiet in the main cabin, when at last I quitted the bridge. It was a long wide saloon and it was any refugee craft with people, who slept uneasily, head to toe, along the sides . . . and the stalwart, 'Mingiss' from Gordonstoun on his blanket on the deck, Dog tight against his side. There was no sound from Raihana's cabin and I imagined they were all sleeping deeply. The Chinese

269

crew were in the engine room and I had peered down into the space below the cabin deck and had been astonished at the spit and polish of engines in perfect condition. There was no evidence here of the neglect of the paint work up top. The engine ran sweetly and there was an extraordinary power about it and the speed was faster than I expected, but then what did I know of seamanship, only knew that in this strange noisy place were three Chinese men and there but for the grace of God, might have worked Fred — small, neat learned men, with slanted eyes and very dark hair too and all very busy, this crew, at the sight of my face at the hatch.

There was a binnacle lamp burning in the cabin and the sighing of river-water brushing against the bow of the ship . . . the throb, throb of engines . . . and a few miles downstream, the no man's land, where we must cross back into Vietnam. I sat down in a corner . . . and in my dreams presently, I heard movement outside the ports and mercifully, the music was still. Then, it must have been hours afterwards, Rat was there and he took my hand in his.

"Time to go on stage, Lady."

It was impossible. It could not be happening. Rat had taken me to somewhere he called the orlop deck, and at least there was privacy.

"The laird will have no hand in this, but I'd like you to remember that you're our passport across the barrier."

On this quiet deck, he handed me a bar of soap and a bucket of clean water. Then he turned his back on me. He had flung a garment over the rail, a scarlet sarong, embroidered with gold dragons.

"Suzy's ruled out of this. They're shooting Chinese on sight. You'll play it solo, you're my Malay girl from Kuala Lumpur. I'd intended Suzy to take part, but she's hidden below and also my crew. They'll have to stay as quiet as dead mice, till we're past the Vietnam border — or they will be dead mice for real, and that's no joke. It's the truth. You and I will be on our own, Lady, and no man will put a hand on you, for you're my woman. There's no danger for you. I would never let you play the part, if there was danger in it. Get washed and put on that sarong, the gold blouse too."

I did as he told me and he turned his back in deference to my modesty and while I washed and re-dressed myself, he spoke almost to himself.

"You're a poor mixed-up kid, you are. I'm a ship's captain — not much of a one but I hold my ticket. If you don't believe in hand fasting, I can make you man and wife legal. All you've got to do is say the word and it will be legal like and there'll be no more tormenting of body and soul . . . "

I doused myself from the bucket of water and used the soap, to free myself from dusty disguise. I washed my hair till it shone like silver and put on the sandals and the red dragoned sarong and the gold blouse. He gasped when he turned round and saw me and then he was captain of himself again and the river had widened with lights up ahead.

"Lights on forward. Lights aft," he called softly and our lights came on and we were held in brilliance.

"Run out the rations. Spike 'em well."

There was a row of barrels that appeared from somewhere and they made a counter, with drinking utensils, of enamel and cups and glasses and drink flowing.

"Prop yourself against the rail there and stay put. You're my new Malay girl. If you stick too close to character, Grant will likely kill us both."

We were running into a wharf and spot lights sought us and found us and the neon came on and the music machine was 'rolling out the barrel' and the whole river had come alive with searching beams. There were small men coming aboard in black battle dress and they drank out of tin mugs and enamel cups. They drank out of bottles. They greeted Rat like an old friend and there was the chink of coins. After a long time they left with a cursory look at the papers and with bottles and gourds and aluminium canteens and with wide smiles . . .

It happened again at the Vietnam line, a replay of this, with the party merrier and the old Indo China of French possession . . . and savoir faire to protect me from any insults, but there were none. I leaned against the rail and drank a great deal of tomato juice, but I said in Malay that it was mostly vodka and that this was a party . . . and God help me, the devil put a potion in their mouths to steal away their brains, so we got through.

It was a long time after, when we were creeping along the dark river again and all was quiet and Rat had partaken of some of his own vintage. It had taken so long . . . so very very long . . . and Rat was a trifle inflamed, with success and his own brew . . . and Gareth and he and I were alone on the dark bridge.

"I'm a Ship's Captain, I am," Rat was telling us. "I have the right to marry anybody, what wants marriage." He took my hand in his and gave it to Gareth and his words slurred a bit.

"If you haven't taken to hand-fasting Lady and I don't blame you, I hereabouts pronounce ye' man and wife," he said . . . "And you're wed as legally as if you were in Westminster Abbey, and maybe you take my cabin for the night . . . "

I declined his offer of the cabin and Gareth was put out with him, yet he had got us safely through danger with no thought that he might be put up against a wall and shot.

"Thank you, Captain Fergusson. It's a nice thought, but I've set my mind on the kirk at Slievenailra," I said. I spent the rest of the night, still in my disguise as a 'Malay hooker' and I wore the sarong till it grew travel stained, and the sandals were comfortable and made better deck wear than Rat's tennis shoes, and soon we were running through the Delta in Vietnam and I was wondering at the versatility of the music, for it ground out tune after tune, with an occasional kick from Rat . . . and I asked myself if it was he, who had made it play 'If you were the only girl in the World . . . ' specially for the most unofficial marriage ceremony I ever hope to see. Still we waited for the kirk at Slievenailra . . . and I asked myself what sort of a fool I was, when Gareth and I ached, one for the other . . . where as much licence existed as it might have been found in Johnny's Bar in Bangkok, if ever there had been such a place.

Slowly we made our way through a traffic jam of small ships towards the Mekong Delta.

There was happiness in this old paddle steamer, for all the misery, that must exist in all our breasts from the memories of what had happened to the nuns at the Convent, from the tragedy of Fred and our sorrow for Suzy's sorrow, from the sight of what was happening in these troubled countries. We had seen people die on the labour camp trek. Now we travelled along the Mekong and surely in all its history, it had never been as it was today?

We kept the music blaring and we got used to it, got used to the sad faces that looked up at us as we went by. We grew accustomed to the jam-packed traffic of refugees in craft of every type and, it seemed, of many nations. Rat had his ports of call, cargo to deliver, cargo to accept for transport, in secrecy. There were small villains, who crept aboard with rice, or coffee, tea, tobacco, sweet potatoes, maybe quinine or cinnamon and left with bottles or kegs.

Constantly we were on our guard against sudden search, but it never came. There were so many craft and the Victoria was no secret vessel. The

Queen Victoria was a familiar sight.

The saloon cabin was our living room and there we played games with the children. As soon as night fell, we fished the river and so we moved on very slowly, with lesser boats making way for us, till we came to the delta, where a river 2800 miles long, discharged the wealth of its silt to the sea, through so many mouths. The Mekong had risen in Tibet. It had passed through the Chinese province of Yunnan, the Shan country, Laos, Cambodia and now Vietnam and this had been Cochin China, but who knew what a country was called from one day to the next? There is no point in describing the vastness of the Delta, this union of land and water, only in saying that Rat knew the way he wanted to go and there he went, without map or compass, turning into a small channel of water here to find another greater stream, then off at a tangent by secret ways, but the Delta held no secrets from him. One day near the going down of the sun, our bows began to rise to the sea. Off shore now, the sun was almost at the horizon and there was a path of gold between it and us. There were islands that were thrown down in the sea like black dice on a golden carpet. There were ships aplenty. There were ships with sails, that looked like so many leaves against the far edge of eternity. The islands were black yet gilt with the sun and there were so many that nobody could thread a path through them. From now on, Rat was on the bridge. He sailed out with a fine carelessness, his eye on three stars, hanging in the sky.

"It used to be the Gulf of Siam. Maybe it's the South China Sea now. It's a long trip and we can't risk rough weather. We take heed of the forecasts from now on. They say the place is as full of pirates as a dog is full of fleas, so we travel by night and hole up by day. They're after the refugees. They have cargo worth plundering . . . and for that matter, so have we."

He smiled at me for he was giving me the pleasure of a turn at the wheel.

"Don't worry, lady. We don't need no lights for navigation now."

The three little girls had formed an attachment to him and they haunted the bridge, whenever they could escape from Raihana. He put them to polishing the brass and scrubbing the deck but nothing deterred them. He was far more lenient than their Amah was. I sometimes wondered why life had denied him the pleasure of being a father, for he would have been one in a thousand. On the spur of the moment, I asked him and he was angry at my impertinence, told me that he had fathered children all over the China Seas and that he did not give a damn what became to any one of them. So he squashed me to silence and then took pity at my hurt face, his hand on my arm.

"I'll not have you think bad of me. I loved a Malay girl once — wedded her in a Temple and all. I was like you, wanted it all done proper and to last. Maybe we offended her god. Oh, she was a sweet one! There was a look of her about you, I thought, that first day I saw you, but of course, you're white, but she was as beautiful, the colour of dark honey and the look of a queen. She give me a babby, but she died and the babby died with her. Maybe

I died myself that day. I sometimes wonder. I'm true to her, always will be, in my own fashion. That first time I saw you, my heart turned over in my chest. It doesn't pay to love one woman all your life. Maybe you'll find that out for yourself and the Laird too. It's a strange old world and we make the best of it . . . try to forget what heaven was like. Now you forget all I just said. You're a fine woman and it will turn out right for you. I'm sure of it, surer than I've ever been of anything. The sight of you gave me the heart to try to do what just ain't possible to do. The sea out there is full of sharks. A man might just as well try to swim it to come to Malaya, yet I know we'll get by. I'll unload my cargo at Penang Island and pick up another and start all over again, and so it goes on."

He looked up at the three stars again and began to talk Malay . . .

"Bulan trang, bintang barchahaya . . . berchahaya burong gaga . . . "

Maybe he forgot I could speak Malay, but I caught it up from him and spoke the translation.

'The moon is clear, the stars shine
  bright above.
The crow is feeding in the rice
  apart.
If thou, my lord, misdoubt my
plight of love,
Come cleave my breast and see my
  wounded heart.'
He was taken aback at that and looked
at me in silence for a long time. Then he
had my shoulders between his hands, as
if he regretted all that might have been.

"The Laird's a lucky man, to have you
by his side for the rest of his life, even if
time runs out on him or on you. He's
had your love and you've had his. I'll do
my best to get y' across the sea and from
Malaya onwards, there'll be no problem.
The future looks so bright for y' both that
maybe we're tempting providence? 'The
best made schemes of mice and men
gang aft agley' . . . and there's plenty
of time yet for tragedy, with tragedy on
every side."

He released my shoulders and took the
wheel over.

"Just for now, there's an island I've got
to nose out, with a creek that strikes deep

into the side of it. We can anchor there to doomsday and the devil himself couldn't find us. We'll lie hid by day. That will be the way. We'll come safe home in the finish. I give you my solemn promise."

He pretended to be concentrating on steering a difficult passage and then lifted a hand to look at his finger nails, as if he told me nothing of importance.

"I know you're worried about Scotland and what's happening in your grandpappy's house and in the Laird's castle. We sent out a signal, that should reach both places. It says that the eagle still flies bravely and that the girl with the black velvet bow is safe and well. It went by a carrier pigeon that knows how to carry a message straight to its destination. He ain't got no feathered wings, but he knew the second world war. Don't go fretting about the worry some people might be having on your behalf. We've come the best part of the way and the most dangerous. Soon you'll be walking the hill to the Castle with the Laird's hand in yours and the rest of it will be just a dream that's gone past."

8

Was it Such an Awfully Big Adventure

WE set out into the China Seas and threaded through the islands that night and Rat might have had an in-built Asdic, with the way he caught the sound of an island and steered safely round it, as if his ear caught an echo from it. There were many craft still and most of them hove-to for the night, but we passed them by. It was an amazing sight, these ships in flight. There were pleasure steamers, such as could ply from London to Margate. There were sampans, and fishing boats, and all were loaded past the safety line with frightened people. We spot lit them a few times, but so terrified, they were, that we stopped giving them any attention, even a friendly hail. They were camped out on deck and it was certain, they were packed like sardines below. They carried all their possessions. At first, Rat spoke to some of them through the hailer, asked them if they needed help, but they wanted none of us. They were bound for Malaya, for Borneo, for Australia, in cockle shell ships, that could never face rough seas. After a while, we steered clear of them. There was nothing we could do and they had anchored for the night. This was difficult navigation. They must move by day, for they had no expert pilot, as we had. There were pirates, who hunted them down. The authorities were their least fear. There were people who would kill them and throw them into the sea for their smallest possessions and here was Rat's shark infested swim.

In the dawn, we found an island as near to heaven, as ever I hope to see. It was wooded and mountainous, with an unblemished white sandy beach, that looked as if no man's foot had ever trod there. We slept by order of our skipper, for we would be on our way at nightfall. He steered the Queen Victoria into a small creek and round a jutting rock into a perfect harbour and there we lay all day. When darkness had come down, we were up anchor and away and Rat with the same uncanny way he had of navigation and so it went on. Then came a storm, but there had been a few days safe passage and now in half an hour, he had us in the lee of another land and was finding anchorage, waiting for the dawn and nosing out a natural harbour.

"We'll lie here till the wind blows itself out."

We were well away from sight of open sea and so we stayed and presently the storm still blowing, we were sent ashore to pass the monotony.

I found myself on a steep slope with Gareth, just as the cool of the evening was coming down. We planned to go a little way up a hill and come down again and we walked hand in hand and we spoke soft words to each other and I know that was what Rat had planned that we do. We must have climbed a mile, through the great trees of the slope, when we came on a deserted village. There were bamboo huts here, but they were long out of use. We wandered through what must have been a small community. It had no inhabitants and the elements had laid it waste. They had had coconut palms. They had grown rubber. They had tried to cultivate nutmegs, but it had all reverted to jungle tangle . . . only for a small house that was built of stone. It was like a child's toy, small and perfect. They must have carried stone up from the shore and mortared them together. The door was made from ship's planks. The windows were open squares. God have mercy! There was a cross at the east gable and it had been painted white, but now it was tangled with a jungle creeper, that gave it beauty and trumpet flowers. The creeper had taken over the roof too and the white trumpets gave the place a vulnerable glory.

There might be snakes and rats inside. It was hot, but I shivered a little, as Gareth opened the door. We walked into the cool of any tropical church at the going down of the sun. The pews were made of ship's planks too just rough wooden benches. The altar had been fashioned from a piece of carved wood, obviously retrieved from the sea. The altar had known loving hands. Somebody had been interested in beachcombing and they had watched and waited. They had found old ships' figureheads and here they were, as trestles to the altar, Mary, the Star of the Sea, supported one side and a handsome Dolphin the other and the crude paint work as fresh and bright as ever.

There was a white linen cloth . . . a chalice, that had been polished . . . polished recently, so there was somebody here, yet there was such complete silence, no sound except the early croaking of the frogs, and the whistle of the storm in the tall trees.

There was a door in the east end of the church, that was set behind the altar and now it began to open, inch by inch. The hair prickled the back of my neck and I groped for Gareth's hand and waited. It could not be possible but there was a man shuffling in to say Benediction. I saw the monstrance in his hand and because I had been interested in all religions since I was knee high to a mouse, I knew it was Benediction and that here was a priest, who carried the monstrance . . . a gold, but more likely a gilt holder on a small stand of similar metal. There would be the small door to it, to admit the Host . . . The God of gods.

The priest looked at us without surprise but with a great gladness, put the monstrance on the altar and took a gilt-gold box from his pocket. He took out a wafer from the box and again I recognised the Holy Catholic Church. Now the wafer was in the monstrance and the man was kneeling in adoration. Then he stood up and turned to face us, holding the monstrance high in triumph.

I had attended the grace of Benediction in great cathedrals, with incense, that smoked prayers to God in vaulted roofs. I had heard hymns that pealed praise against stained glass windows, had seen gold-coped bishops, surrounded by humble acolytes, but never do I hope to see such humility and faith and belief, as I felt now.

"I knew, if I waited, my children would come back to me." he said in French. "I'm padre here, have been for a long time."

Here was a man of great patience and wisdom, who would hold a pass till he was the last soldier left, aye and beyond that. He said no more to us, just bid us welcome and read a few prayers, but he apologised to God for his haste, spoke to him man to man.

"Lord God, it's just that it was so long till they came!"

Then the service was over and we were in the room where he lived behind the church, invited to take meat with him.

"I have hens and a good cow. I have the sea below and like the disciples, I am a good fisher."

Here was a lamp-lit living room behind the chapel with furniture made from the jetsam of the ocean. He sat us down and made us welcome and he invited us to tell what had brought us. Perhaps he had better begin by telling us about himself. He was an old man but we could see that. He wore a tattered soutane and he apologised about that. His hat was a French Priest's biretta and he was dark in the jowl, but turning to white in the head. He had had a parish here in Cochin China, but it was all changed now. They had left him, every one of his flock, but not willing to go. They had been taken away to work on the mainland, but he was too old. They had not wanted him and they had knocked him senseless and left him for dead, but it was not God's will. When he was a young man, he had had his first parish in a small village in France, but he had thought it a great honour to become a missionary, not that he had caught as many souls as he might have imagined possible.

He was convinced that the good Lord had kept him alive for some task. It had been a long time to live like Monsieur Crusoe. But at last, we had come. He had the French inflection in his voice, but he had diagnosed us as English speaking, so now he spoke English and all his sentences finished uphill and he had that French élan about him still and he pronounced 'Phnom Penh' as only a Frenchman can.

I could not believe the scene was real. We were talking together as if we were life-long friends . . . this small, bright-eyed man in the tattered garments of God's missionaries. He had my sort of philosophy, that there was one God and that all Gods were one. He and I had a conversation that could not be real about

Confucius and about Aesculapius and about the Snake Temple at Penang and it took me straight back down the years to Grandfather in Glenmore. Presently we were on the subject of Slievenailra and all about how Gareth and I loved each other and were trying to swim like salmon up a weir . . . how we wanted to get wed in the kirk on the mountain . . . and how precarious was our journey.

We begged him to come down to the ship and travel with us. We knew that his parish was a dream of the past and that never again would he speak to his flock in that French intonation and with the graceful dramatic gestures and the uptilt of every sentence at the finish.

He would never desert his church and we were hoping that Rat was not out of his mind with worry about what was delaying us, but we had hit on a small miracle — no, in no way small — a great glorious miracle of faith and belief. Hour after hour, we stayed talking and we ate shrimps caught from the sea that morning, served with rice, very like the 'shrimps with rice', that had been my passion in the days of my childhood and I marvelled at the path-way of life.

We went into the Church, before we said goodbye and he gave us his blessing and he gave us a small parchment to keep safely, told us to keep it all our lives. He signed it Alexandre!

Then it was all over and we both wondered, if it had ever happened. We stood before Rat on the bridge and heard what he had to say about the length of time we had been gone and no signal from us.

Then we lay together and loved each other. We slept like the dead and in the morning we knew we had wandered into a dream of paradise, into a world that never existed, into a place we could never find again.

Tomorrow we might walk up the same hill and there would be no church. If we looked for a thousand years, we would never again find that small, humble, holy house nor the priest with the faded tattered cassock and the French tilt to his voice and his eyes black and bright as elderberries. It was a mirage in a desert, a trick of time and space. The storm was stilled to calm the next evening, and that night we put to sea again and went on across the shark-infested waters and no shark is as cruel as man can be and so we found it.

There had been no excuse to stay on the island, for the storm had passed. We did not dare to climb the hill again in case we found nothing, then indeed we would have been expelled from Eden. We headed out into the swell, negotiated what had been known as the Point de Camau, but a name was important no more. Now there were fewer ships and south west of us was Kota Bharu, and well I knew Kota Bharu in Malay. Rat told us he intended to steer for it and then hug the coast line of Malaya, go south round Singapore and then north to Penang Island where the Temple of Snakes was. It was the way he always went. His ship would not be questioned and he had customers en route and he would land us in Kota Bharu, if we liked, but we were welcome to stay with the ship for the whole voyage. He knew a man on Penang Island, in Georgestown, who would personally see to our flight home . . . and surely home was the Castle of Slievenailra on Turnish! The matter of the hostages could be sorted out with no publicity in the world.

Gareth and I dwelt in Arcady. I can remember every minute of every hour of that journey. There were fugitive ships still, and we passed them by. Then one night, reality caught up with us. There was a strange craft astern and gaining on us and it presently sent a stream of automatic fire across our bows and bid us stand to. There was nothing to do but obey. It comes back to my mind, as clearly as it was that night, when Rat caught the old life boat in a spot from the bridge. It had done duty in some British seaside town in its good days, but now it was pirate craft. There were automatic rifles that covered us and men that were not men, but beasts, with close-shaven heads and slanted eyes. Here then, were the pirates, who preyed on the refugees and this could only be the end of our voyage. Rat stood on the bridge and looked down on them and the cigarette still on his lower lip, the wry smile, the white topped captain's cap and the gold braid. It was all over between one moment and the next. He held a grenade in his hand and the pin out of it. It went across the stretch of water into the centre of the life boat and there was an explosion and men flung in all directions — in rags and in tatters of men — men, who would have killed us. Then we had switched off all lights and were on our way and Rat was the king of the seas, another grenade in his fist, as he waited for them to come on again, but they were gone off into the darkness and the expanse of the sea.

"Don't weep for them, lady. They'd have cut our throats and fed us to the sharks. They've even taken to making their captives walk the plank. There are plenty more where they came from, but it's no cause for alarm. We have a locker of grenades against them and I've run out of mercy. God forgive me! We'll just have to take care. They hunt in packs and there are wolves will want our blood for theirs — and our women and our cargo. I don't know why they're so hot to get me. I'm an honest trader, I am. Ask anybody from Penang Island to Phnom Penh. They'll tell you there's no harm in me."

He looked at me sideways with a grin and I knew that he didn't give a damn and yet I wondered. I thought of his honey-skinned Malayan wife, remembered 'Bulan trang, bintang barchahaya . . . the moon is clear, the stars shine bright above . . . come cleave my breast and see my wounded heart . . . ' Here was a puzzle indeed. He had sacrificed his ship and himself and his honest cargo, just to get us home. I took his hand in mine and laid my lips against the back of it and have always been glad that I did so.

Now we were forging ahead at full steam, regardless of all other craft and he never quitted the bridge. At dawn, there was a small fleet of ships astern, coming up fast and he did not like it. He circled an island and I have pencilled it many times since. I drew it for one authority after another. It was etched on my brain, but no name to it. We circled it slowly and so got out of sight of the small fleet and it did not take much intelligence to guess that here was the rest of the pirate fleet. We circled the island and found a deep cove and Rat nosed out a place with good cover from the sea. We moored at daybreak, but there was a slight chance of us being found. In case we were, Grant had made his plans. If they came ashore, we were to lie hidden. There must be no sound from the Queen Victoria and no smoke, no going ashore. There was a headland opposite and he would lie there on observation and he would draw them off. If they landed, he would play the part of a bird with her nestlings. There had been a report on the radio that morning that the authorities were seeking an Englishman, who was reported to be travelling illegally and holding hostages for ransom. They had even got our position fairly accurately, though I was not sure of the identity of the authorities. The Englishman had murdered defenceless women in a convent in the border country and had gone on to massacre honourable officers of the Republic. He had taken hostages, but the Republic would never let him leave the territory. It fitted. How well it fitted!

Gone are the days, when the British can sail up the Mekong in a gun boat and shell the empty city of Phnom Penh! The British sun has sunk below the horizon and another sun is going up the sky . . .

Rat Fergusson bit his underlip.

"We have the pirates, right on our tail and we have the honourable soldiers of the Republic of Kampuchea for good measure, the small men in black battledress, who killed those nuns themselves . . . and who killed Suzy's man and all the passengers on that plane . . . and if anybody noses us out, it will be the pirates. They'll search every crevice in this coastline and they might come in here. If the soldiers try for us, they'll go inland and set ambush."

"The Laird will lead them off," Menzies said. "We used to go on chases at Gordonstoun, just to toughen us. It was bloody murder, but it was fun if you survived it, like the cold showers on the edge of the Arctic."

We could see Grant high on the crag, that was like one of his own eagle's eyries. In mid morning, he stood up and lit his pipe, signalled to us that the craft were on their way.

"Here they come," Rat muttered. "The Laird will lead them off."

We saw it all. It was played on a backcloth of silvered wooded mountain that was not unlike some of the mountains behind Glenmore. They came ashore at the other side of a headland and they trekked up the steep path towards where he stood and presently he had gone. Then I saw that Rat was uneasy. He had his glasses on the mountain and he had seen something, that dismayed him very much. I took the glasses from him, though he was unwilling to part with them and presently I found out what he had seen. Here was a three-cornered war, as it always seems to be these days. There was ambush that might have been set for the pirates, who were following Gareth. I knew well the small black battledressed men with the deadly fire power. They must have been after us perhaps or perhaps after the pirate craft. They had landed before them maybe they were after us. We shall never know. They were higher up the mountain, in a cleft in the hill. They had complete superiority of position and Grant was leading the pirates up and up, straight into the trap. There was nothing we could do. I might shout myself hoarse, but my voice was stolen by the noise of the sea, by the distance, by the screaming of disturbed sea birds. Gareth was a stag hunter. He knew how to lead men up a mountainside, but he did not know he led them to their death and his own. He must be first in the line of fire. They came after him like so many creeping wolves, like a raggle taggle of careless gypsies, the shorn heads and the slanty eyes and the pirate look to them, and knives flashing the sun. We heard the rifle fire too clearly and now they had all disappeared from the stage . . . only one short sharp savage battle and sounds rebounding from crag to crag and then silence . . . such silence that I heard only the wash of the sea against the hull.

"You can't be sure, lady. He ain't a fool. He'll have seen that the little men were in ambush. He'll lie doggo. We'll stand by to repel boarders and if he doesn't come back soon, we'll go on recce, up the mountain."

He made me wait all day and I hope never to live out so long a day again. Two hours before sun down, we set out to find him, but before that, we had moored the Queen Victoria hard under a cliff and covered her with the camouflage of the branches of trees. Then we found a cave and hid what Rat called the vulnerable personnel. He was ex-navy surely for his speed and efficiency. The three Chinese crew and the Little Hopper were to stay in a cave . . . and no sound out of them . . . and Raihana and the three little sheikesses too. He went below to the galley and he packed their rations with his own hands at double speed. He shoved a package lunch into Raihana's hands.

"It may have to last a bit. *Make* it last. There are two enemies and the Chinese must stay with you. Their lives are forfeit and your three children are ransom bait — and the boys also. Was there ever such an ill begot crew? I'm taking the lady and I'm taking Suzy even though Suzy's Chinese. She's got medical knowledge and we're going to need all we have. There's been a war on up there on the slopes. If you see anybody strange, not a sound out of you and that's it. It's no nonsense. It's a matter of your lives."

He stood opposite Suzy and told her if the troops were Vietnamese they'd likely shoot her on sight and she was proud with him.

"You are thinking I care, if they shoot me?"

Suzy and Rat and I climbed up the steep wooded side of a mountain, up to the place where Grant had stayed in hiding, up to the ridge from which he had drawn the pirates after him but he had not been able to see the ambush that waited. We found the remnants of battle in a small hollow, over the top of a hill. The grass was black with mourning for the dead and they lay flung down like rag dolls . . . so many of them, mostly the patchwork of the pirates, but some of the black battledress of Kampuchea too. Out at sea, they were steaming away, the official boat and the pirate craft too and neither of them interested in the other any more. They had gone off like fighting surly curs to lick their wounds.

Rat saw him first and he grabbed me into his arms and held me closely, refused to let me go free and Suzy had gone from us and was back again.

"Missie, I am so sorry to tell you and my heart is breaking. The Tuan is dead. There is no doubt of it. I know the clothes he wore. I know the crested ring on his finger — even his white handkerchief in his side pocket and the Little Hopper's glasses. I have learnt how to identify death as you have but never did it bring me more sorrow and him you must not see. Never . . . never . . . never . . . just remember how he was . . . "

He was lying by a small hillock and his injuries were awful. He was a heap of old clothes and I had seen such casualties. This was war and I cradled him in my arms and could not weep. They were digging a shallow grave and we made him as decent as we could and I pretended to myself that he was a casualty in the hospital and that I did not know him from any stranger.

He had died of multiple injuries from gun-shot wounds. That was the verdict . . . identifiable only by his clothing and by the ring on his finger. God have mercy on him! He had been shot to bits and detail is no help to sorrow.

The grave was shallow. Suzy and Rat dug it and I gathered wild orchids and wondered how I could survive such a blow. In one minute, my life was over, I had lost all I possessed and I wanted to die myself, but the ones that might have dealt out such mercy to me had gone sailing off across the sea. Now there was a small cross to make and I made it of two broken branches of some fragrant trees. What was the point of putting on it that here lay the Eagle of Slievenailra? I was a dead woman and I had no feeling, only an emptiness. I took the ring from his finger and could not see it clearly. It belonged on my finger now but what was the future worth . . . not two dead sparrows in the dust of a gutter. I went off down the hill, after Rat had said some sort of prayer about death at sea. They followed me after a while, respecting the silence, that had come on me.

"They butchered each other, the pirates and the soldiers . . . not many of them left. He got caught in the cross-fire and he gave his life to draw both lots away from the children and us."

They might have been talking to a corpse, so much I heeded them. There we were near the sea and near enough the cave, where the others lay hidden.

"Don't tell them," I whispered. "Say we found nothing and that it's all over. It's no good making children cry."

"Missie is lost for him," Suzy said. "He's hidden out in the hills and we can't find him. One day, she'll find him again and then we will all be glad."

It was the best face to put on it. I was frozen solid in sorrow, amazed that I could feel no pain . . . only a great void. As I had cared for Suzy, so now she cared for me, always at my side, always within call, always with love in her heart for me, her hand to lead me. So we went on across the China Seas and Malaya was in sight and Kota Bharu and here with the home-land in my eyes, I started to weep and thought I might never leave off, for these were my people, though they were not his people. Here lay my father and mother and my grandfather and grandmother. Here had been my childhood and Malaya put out her arms and took me home.

I had hidden my tears. I had waited till my eyes were not burnt holes in blankets, as Suzy had said to my child self in those old happy days. Then I had found Rat alone on the bridge.

"I'd like you to put me ashore here. In a way, I've come home . . . "

He looked at me and took in the full picture and tilted his cap more over his eyes, did me honour by flicking his cigarette overboard, almost unsmoked.

"We're safe now, lady. There'll be no more pirates, no more soldiers."

I asked him savagely if I cared much for pirates or soldiers and he smiled gently at me.

"I'd like you to stay aboard with me, till the Snake Temple at Penang. It's an idea I have and I'd be pleased if you'll see out the voyage. I can make it smoother for you. I'm almost sure I can and I'm an honest seaman. I think there may be something I know that you haven't realised yet. Just give me a little time to make this trip bearable for you. I know that's impossible seen from where we stand now, but I've set my heart on doing the impossible just one time more . . . thought I was beaten a while back, but these last few days, I've wondered, when I've seen your face in the dawning. I'll drop anchor here and I'll go ashore. I'll send the news on to Scotland. I know you think it's your job, but I'll make it mine. They can put up a fine brass plate in the kirk and send his piper out to lament the hills, for his loss but that's not the end of him. I mind you going down the hill that day and you leaving a cross for him. I stayed back to put a name on the grave. It might comfort you to know that he lies under a wooden cross. A sailor gets used to whittling at wood. 'Here lies Gareth Grant, The Laird of Slievenailra on Turnish.' That's what I wrote on it . . . 'the swiftest Eagle of them all . . . ' They can put the same words on a brass plate in the kirk, but it won't match the sweet cross you put over him, with the smell of Rosemary . . . of the remembrance of your love for him.

Branches of a tree it was, but I know nothing of trees."

He took the oily cloth from his back pocket and thought to blow his nose on it. Then he knew it was no handkerchief and drew his sleeve across his face, thought to turn off his emotion like a tap and failed completely, for he went on.

"If you'd do me a favour and let me run your life for a bit and don't forget that I know how you feel this minute. Suzy's known it too. Take a few more weeks off. Give the Lord a bit of extra time to ban what He done."

I wanted to weep again. I could not speak to refuse him, so I just nodded my head and left the bridge and went below to play Pelmanism with the three little girls and did not find one matching pair, and the days ran slowly as molasses poured in winter, but with no sweetness. The matched pairs had all run out, quite inexorably.

It's useless to prolong the story at this point. Rat fixed it in that casual way he had. There were Embassy officials who came aboard and talked to me. There were cables that rocketed out across the world. There were planes, zooming in from the north and from south and from east and from west. Came a day, with Rat on the bridge with myself, when we saw the fleet of white Mercedes cars arrive on the dock below us. There was a passenger in the first car and his garments whiter than the cars. The scarlet band round his brow, showed that he was the Lord of his creation, that, and the way the others bowed down to him as if he were an idol. They quitted the cars and approached the Queen Victoria and got permission to come aboard and presently just below the bridge on deck, their father was united with the three little 'sheikesses'. He must have owned half the oil kingdoms of the Middle East, must have possessed the power of Attila, the Hun, over his own subjects but on board the Queen Victoria, Rat was Captain. The three little girls were produced with Raihana and Raihana on her knees at once. The entourage knelt to the children, who had been nothing but a trio of spoiled brats. Maybe there was wonder that the children ran up the companionway and begged to be allowed to stay with Rat. They clung to his frayed trouser legs and gently he put them aside and they trooped forlornly back to all the splendid young men in white garments. They wept to be allowed to stay on the old paddle steamer. They said that they had been so happy . . . and the court knelt to the children at the bottom of the companion way, when they bade farewell to the Captain. Up there, he was the king of the world and I knew it and they knew it. The father began to speak of rich rewards and Rat tossed his cigarette into the sea.

"We didn't do it for gold. I hadn't much choice in it, but if they had been from the slums of the Gorbals, they were children and children are our future and children and children . . . "

They promised rich gifts and then bowed their graceful way off the ship with the three little girls and with Raihana and we were so much the poorer. It all made no impression on my sorrow. I might have been a marble statue for all the ceremony impressed me, but I knew I had wandered into a sad film show, that made me close to tears. Soon the light would go on and I might be caught unawares, in a day-light reality of shame and sorrow.

Jenny and the she-goat were collected by some Malayan nuns, who surrounded her with the adoration of the Magi. They wanted to take the donkey too, but Rat was determined not to part with 'old Ned', as he always called Fanny. "The donkey was mine," he said. "I might want it in Slievenailra. It would have a good home and I might want it for transport" — and never could I have understood what he meant by that.

They departed, one by one, with a typical Scots gentleman, collecting the Little Hopper. Fraser had the glasses back on his nose and all steamed up with tears. I could not forget how I had come on the glasses in that shot-up coat and the Little Hopper was ashamed of his tears, till I put Donald into his arms and then he hugged me as if he never wanted to leave me and could hide his tears no more.

"This is Donald, who lays eggs," I told his father and we all managed a very false laugh and they were gone.

A typical Scots laird collected Menzies and Dog and spoke to me about Grandfather. I bent my head and stroked the lurcher, valued the wag of his tail beyond all human gratitude. There was no gratitude owing to me and I wanted none. I was glad, when they had all gone and the planes were winging their way out to their homes from my beloved peninsula. I was on the Queen Victoria, with the three Chinese crew, with Rat and with Suzy and with the donkey and the engines were running sweetly and we were nosing out to sea. Soon we were running at full steam, south, along the coast of Malaya. The news of our adventures had gone over the media to the whole world and it was time for us to be up and away.

I was alone on the bridge the night we left — only for Rat at the wheel. The sunset was a glory, and he looked at the sky moodily. "Maybe I'll not stop doing impossible things," he said, and after a while, "I was thinking the way you had the words for it . . . in English, I mean 'The moon is clear the stars shine bright above,

The crow is feeding in the rice
  apart.
If thou, my lord, misdoubt my plight
  of love . . . '
It came over me of a sudden what I told
you. Maybe it pays to love one woman
all your life, but I reckon maybe I was
wrong. Maybe it can happen all over
again . . . "

Suzy appeared on the bridge with three
cups in her hand on a gold tray. They
were a gift from Arabia and I imagine
that the china was gold-precious, from
Minton or Rockingham. They were full
of some drink, that I thought might be
tea and I was in another world, not
caring much if I drank it or not. I
could not gather what Rat was trying
to tell me. I still gnawed on it like a
dog with a bone. Meanwhile, I took the
cupful in one draught and was back in
the scorched plains with Rat's own drink
from Johnny's Bar in Bangkok in my
stomach . . . and me, hag-ridden with
fever, awaiting the delivery of Jenny's
baby. This drink, taken in one great
gulp, lit me up like a torch, hit my
stomach and sent rockets up across my

sky. I gasped for air and the breath I dragged into my lungs was molten fire, so that I beat my chest with a clenched fist. Rat took a drink from his cup and the delicate china looked incongruous against the tough tan of his seaman's face.

"Rum," he said and tried it again, looked at Suzy with approval. "It might be best to put more water in it," he said gently.

There was a tiny piece of my personal jigsaw, that slotted into place, and Suzy had known it best to put tea in her own cup. She had got the rum from the holy nuns that came aboard to fetch Jenny and the baby. It had been marked 'For medicinal purposes only' and another circle turned full.

We were rounding Singapore well out to sea, and Suzy stayed on the bridge. The great port was something she must see. One day, Rat promised her she would take the wheel. Then we were turning north along the peninsula again and here was Penang Island and one day or two days gone. I was not feeling well. I had lost my wish for food and I thought it possible that I might mercifully pine and die. Always, I had been hungry for breakfast, but now I turned my head away. I was a physician and I could not diagnose what was wrong. I was deadly sick in the morning. We anchored at Georgestown, Suzy advised me to take no heed of it.

"You've been under mental trauma, Missie. This I think is a natural sickness. It will go away, but maybe it is time to see a doctor . . . a physician must not try to heal herself."

I wondered if sorrow stopped the course of a woman's life and forgot all I had learnt in the Royal College. The doctor was Chinese. Rat recommended him and I went to see him and presently he was telling me that he was sad for my sorrow, but glad for my great joy. He knew my story. The whole world knew it. I dreaded the cameras, that might appear in Great Britain as soon as I arrived there, but one day I must face Slievenailra and Turnish. I dreaded Slievenailra. My feet could never travel the path up the rise to the Castle . . . never face meeting his people and telling them what I had to tell them, most of which they knew already, or I imagined they did, but I had let them find out from the media. I had not seen the British papers, but I could picture the headlines.

'HEIR TO SLIEVENAILRA OF THE ISLES BUTCHERED BY GUERRILLA TROOPS AND PIRATES IN THE CHINA SEAS . . . A LONELY ISLAND GRAVE . . . '

Maybe the brass plate was on the kirk wall . . . TO THE MEMORY OF GARETH GRANT, LAIRD OF SLIEVENAILRA ON TURNISH . . . THE SWIFTEST EAGLE OF THEM ALL.

Had not Rat written it for them? The newspapers would have made good publicity out of the story . . . and it had happened what seemed a hundred years past.

The Chinese doctor was very old, very wise. He talked to me as one colleague to another, although I was only a *lady* doctor, and he had never heard of the liberation of women.

"It may be that I am mistaken. Strange things happen in battle and a lie says the truth, but this one thing is true. You see I read the papers, but this is not known

316

yet. My lady will bear a child . . . an eaglet for the Tuan Lord of Slievenailra. Your Tuan will never die now. I would like you to think well in this matter and to have wisdom, that your Lord cannot die . . . he will just take a step into the past and be honourable ancestor . . . and the eagles will come back to that island, that is now so famous in the whole world. They will circle the tower of his castle and it will one day be this child's inheritance . . . the eagles will fly again, as soon as you put out your hand to open the door and go into the great hall for has not the new Laird returned to his home?"

He was not dead, not blotted out to nothing. His son lay safe with me and God had been kind. It would have mattered so much to Gareth to know that it had not been the end. I must travel to Scotland. I must visit Glenmore. I must bring the good news to my grandfather and after a while, I must seek out the castle.

I remembered the church on the mountain. I remembered the padre, Paul Alexandre. I remembered the monstrance

317

and last of all, I recalled the parchment with his name signed across it. We had been joined together in holy matrimony according to the rules of the French Church, Gareth and I. When I had held his shattered body in my arms, this had been the one knowledge, that had kept me sane. Death might part us for a time, but it could have no dominion over us. I had lain with him and now I might bear his heir . . . a child, who would have the right to go up the stairs to the gallery on Christmas Eve and fix the star on the Tree . . . a child, who would go climbing the mountain and see to the cutting of the Yule log. Later on, he would read the lessons in church . . . bow his proud head to the Queen's Majesty, when she came to open the Highland Games. He could beget sons and these children could beget sons. The line would run down the years and even if my future must be lonely for Gareth, I had memories, that would never be forgotten . . . memories of how it had been, when I had lain in his arms on the deck of an old steamer with the tropical night a blaze of stars above us.

The voice of the old doctor broke in on my thoughts gently.

"You are a fine memsahib. The British Raj will die with women such as you are. I think, in all life, you will never be replaced. Another nation may reflect from you and American peoples are trying to do it. If America fails, there will be nothing of greatness left to the world, only to spin out into space and become a planet of the apes."

9

The Inheritance

I HAD packed my kit, yet like the three little girls, I did not want to leave the Queen Victoria. Suzy was ready to accompany me, and I knew she would rather have stayed aboard. There was something between Rat and Suzy that I could sense, but not know of a surety.

"It's only that he needs me more than you need me, Missie. Your people are my people, but the time may come, when you will have no more need for me. It is then that the Captain will seek me out. He is a very honourable man and I might steer his ship straighter than he does it himself, but it will be written into the future, not for now. I will be Amah to your baby, till the day you let me go free. There is a long time to life yet and now we have to get the donkey to the island in Scotland and this the Sheik sent an emissary to say it is easy to do. It will all be done, when you want it done. You have just to command and he will obey, like the genie in the Arabian nights."

There were planes at my disposal and secrecy. There was a helicopter there, if I raised my hand. It happened so quickly that I had no belief that it was happening and that I was standing in Turnish, Suzy, donkey and all, at the gates of Slievenailra Castle.

Rat had been sorry to say goodbye to us and ever since his words were wandering round my brain.

"There's talk in the Gulf . . . about a man, who saw a child's hat in the tide and thought a ship lost — that it wasn't lost after all. It was a round straw hat he knew well. I don't put much faith in rumours. A body is a body is a body, be it just a suit of clothes and a boy's specks in the pocket and a ring on a finger, but the nails were dirty. I thought of that after . . . a long time after . . . The nails were dirty, and the Laird's nails were never dirty."

My puzzling was a cat's cradle of string and meant nothing. Surely it could not be that he hinted that Gareth still lived! If he had survived that day, he might have been picked up . . . might be on his way back to the Mekong Delta, with the whole game laid out to play again and it was quite, quite impossible. Yet now when I looked up into the Island sky, the eagles were soaring round the mountain tops and I had not turned the handle of the castle door and put my foot on the floor of the great hall, looked up at the gallery where the eldest son must stand one day, to set the Christmas star in place . . .

A man could dress himself up in another man's clothes and pretend to be dead, when he had much to live for, but it was an impossible dream. I must put it out of my mind.

We left our kit at the gate and walked up the avenue with the donkey between us, Suzy and I, and my hand rested on the cross, as it always did and still my thoughts went up and about my head like Chinese fire crackers.

Gareth might have known that Cambodia was searching for an Englishman. He might have put his clothes on a dead soldier and forgotten all about the Little Hopper's spectacles. He might even have left them as a false trail, together with the crested ring on a dead finger with dirty fingernails. Last night at Glenmore, Grandfather had received me with such love and such concern, yet with triumph.

It was a long grassy slope to the great door of the keep and it was no use starting to create dreams, that could never be. Yet always the thought crept back into my mind. The soldiers might have fought it out with the pirates and Gareth might have realised that the soldiers were after us. He might have disguised himself in a dead man's battle dress, when they had all gone away, leaving the dead. If they came back, they would know that they had killed the Englishman they sought, who was worse than any pirate. His own clothes were on a dead man . . . and the ring. They would loot a body and find a ring and a pair of spectacles. Then there had been nothing at the foot of the hill but a straw hat floating in on the tide. "But I have dreamed a dreary dream beyond the Isle of Skye. I saw a dead man win a fight — and I think that man was I." From the height, he might have seen a ship go down. There were many such. For a long time, he might have wandered round — been picked up at last. He might have travelled many sea miles, before he reached a port — and it was all fantasy. Surely I must be content with motherhood and write off happiness, yet I pictured him in some Far East town with a newspaper in his hand, finding the impossible headlines in a week-old British paper and if he did, he would go to Slievenailra, knowing that I would go there. He knew . . . had known I was his legal wife, but he would not know about his heir. There were only a very few, who knew that. No! No! No! No! It was an impossible dream, of what might have been.

We had left our transport at the bottom of the hill. There was a man who paced the battlements of the tower and piped a lament to the skies and I pushed aside all my false hopes and turned into the little grey kirk and there I came face to face with reality, for there was a brass plate, newly set on the wall and it dazzled my eyes to tears, with its brightness. TO THE MEMORY OF GARETH GRANT, LAIRD OF SLIEVENAILRA ON THE ISLAND OF TURNISH . . . THE SWIFTEST EAGLE OF THEM ALL, DIED IN BATTLE, 1978. HE GAVE HIS LIFE THAT OTHERS MIGHT LIVE . . .

I walked back to join Suzy and thought it a strange thing that I was wearing the same type of clothes I had worn the day he drove to Glenmore with his two shooting dogs in the back of the family car. There had been one golden labrador and one black, sitting up in the back seat of a silent car. They had looked like two dignified old gentlemen. I got a vivid picture of myself with the black velvet ribbon on my hair, with the Royal Stuart kilt and the black sweater with the high roll neck. The lament of the piper tore my dreams to shreds and the tatters of glory echoed back to me from the mountain and I knew that motherhood was no substitute for a life in this place with my husband at my side.

"It is bad for the baby if you grieve all over again," Suzy said softly and I turned on her fiercely and told her that I would grieve all the days of my life. Then I remembered that her sorrow was mine and she had shown great courage. I made no effort to go on up the hill and take the knocker in my hand . . . to turn the round iron handle and go in. I stood outside the kirk and tried to come to terms with life. At least, I was bringing them good news. They should be out on the steps to welcome me and this was a strange greeting, this heart-break lament from the steep of the tower . . . this empty-seeming house and the eagles dropping down from the skies to look at my forlorn self, lone, lone, lone. They came like thunderbolts and I thought they looked at me and wheeled away again — and they carried glory in their wings, but glory was no good to me. There was a car coming up the drive, as fine and finer than the Sheik's cars and it made no sound. I could only hear the baying of dogs and I spun round and saw the castle door open and the two dogs, that came rushing down the grassy hill. The car paused a moment and they leaped in to the back seat, like trained acrobats and after a deal of welcome, they set themselves into position like two elderly gentlemen in the back seat.

There was a man at the wheel in a moleskin jacket with leather patches on the shoulder for the butt of a rifle . . . a man with hair that was fairer from the scorch of the sun, with a sun tanned face.

It was not possible that it had happened, as I had dreamed, but that had been the way of it. He had not known that I was alive, till a few days ago. He was out of the car in one bound and I was close against his chest.

"Virginia," he whispered. "Virginia . . ." and then in Gaelic, in that soft tongue that was surely made for loving, he went on with the rest of it, soft and lilting, heart of his heart, his sweet white dove . . . and a confused ramble of ships lost at sea and a straw hat that floated in the tide, how he had not cared if ever he came home, if I were not to be with him . . . Suzy stopped him at last and told him what she had just told me that this was in no way good for the baby . . . and I thought it a strange thing the way Suzy and myself

327

had had the Gaelic from my grandfather in Glenmore.

He started all over again and then he thought of Suzy's warning and he looked at us as we stood there, with the donkey.

"The remnants of the Holy Family," he said. "And all of us safe home. It's time we went inside and told them, that the piper should be screaming a welcome against the mountain. This lament is for myself and I daresay they played it in your honour. The hall inside will be full of mourning folk and it's a pity to let sorrow go on when it's over and done with. Isn't it a strange thing the way animals have more sense than people?"

The Labradors were fussing about our legs and I reminded him of the day he had come to Glenmore with them and he was sad for a moment and told me that these were not the same dogs. "They're sons, who took over from their fathers and they'll have sons . . . and I will too. It's a strange instinct, animals and birds have. Even the eagles flew down from the skies to look at my bride and bid her welcome and the dogs carried it too and there's 'the old Ned' waiting for a warm stable and a bran mash and maybe presently a small boy to ride on her back when the time's right."

He put his arm round Suzy and I knew even with her face imperturbable that she was not far from tears.

"You'll stay with me, Suzy, just for a little while," I said. "But it's time you went free. It's in my mind that there's a man, who waits for you and he saved all our lives. Maybe in a wee while, you'll take the wheel for him . . . steer your craft to happiness."

Then came the day that starts this story, when I sat in the kirk and the Laird in at the seat next the aisle and Suzy between us with the child we called 'Number One Son', in her arms and he coming in to be baptised. The kirk was packed to the doors. Suzy had waited to be nurse to me, but presently, she would fly away across the ocean to the man that waited for her.

So Number One Son, we called him that day, yet I could look on down the years.

Number Two Son might come in time

329

and he would be no less important in the eyes of the true god but then there are so many gods.

Maybe five years from now, we would be in this same kirk again and Number One Son old enough to have seen a cockroach. I might remember that cockroaches were considered sacred in Vietnam and maybe the boy would have an empty matchbox, in his pocket. There! It was prisoner and this would not please the Laird who knew what a prison was like. I might smile to myself as I saw the cockroach set free to wander off down the aisle and how Number One Son might have learned too much sense to question the judgement. Perhaps it might be Number One Daughter. Yes, that was more like it . . .

Now I turned my eyes to the kirk wall, to the space that was always to spin me back down the years. I do not know why we had not made the wall good, but it was history in a sort of way, the black holes, the screws had left.

I had just to close my eyes and be back there again and I knew that the memory would never fade, of that day when I was ill and when I knew that Jenny's baby was soon to be born. If we had not had the donkey, we could never have come so far. This was an awful place and the nuns had trusted me and Dog licked my hand. I was ill. Some of the time, that night, I had thought it was Christmas night and that shepherds were watching their sheep. I had thought that the whole world was on tip-toe for the birth of Christ and for the coming of Christmas Day. We had gone staggering across the arid plain and then had come the sound of an engine that stuttered and died and a man's voice, that I knew so well now had remarked that maybe he had run out of petrol but probably it was only the plugs. I remembered the open jeep the tattered khaki slacks, the straw hat tilted over his eyes and how he had smiled at me as I stood at the donkey's head . . . then how he had taken in Jenny and the small woebegone faces.

"Hello there, Holy Family! Are you really there or are you some sort of a mirage?"

He had gone off one day and come back with a goat, a brown goat in full milk, with a white beard, and white legs.

If I had to do it again, I would have done it all over again, the same way. In the nights now, I remember all that happened and know that I have a debt that I can in no way hope to repay. Gareth Grant could have gone on his way. I know I found something without price . . . something immortal . . . Rat Fergusson could have refused inflammable cargo, but he did not pass by.

It will soon be time for Suzy to take the child along the aisle to the font, for the minister is waiting for us, yet still I am caught up in the time that has gone and I think of the lonely hill on the small island in the vast continent that is Indonesia. I think of the flat boards that form a cross on a grave, that should be safe from predatory animals, because somebody thought fit to cover it well with rocks against the buzzards and the jackals . . . and in crayon thought to write 'HERE LIES THE SWIFTEST EAGLE OF THEM ALL.'

Maybe the storms and the rains

have not wasted the grave. They will certainly have blown away my wreath of fragrant branches, but the title was wrong, although maybe only emptiness is left. The inscription should have been a different one, for the Laird did not lie there. I bow my head and thank God that this is so, yet I worry about the inscription and the minister waiting to receive my child into Christianity. It should have read HERE LIES AN UNKNOWN SOLDIER. HE IS KNOWN ONLY UNTO HIS GOD . . . . Somewhere there may be a woman, who mourns for him, who waits for him. Her, I always include in my prayers, if she did exist. Every man is entitled to his beliefs and all Gods are one God.

My grandfather is getting very impatient with my delay for, of course, he is present today. He frowns along the pew at me and the Laird is getting to his feet. There is anxiety in his eyes, that I am away to my dream world again. Suzy is standing too and it is time to put the past behind me but this I will never do. Number One Son is fast asleep and he has no knowledge that one day, the eagles will fly for him, that soon, he will be old enough to lean over the balcony and fix the Star of Christmas on the tree, so I go walking along the aisle, with my hand on the Laird's arm and still my heart is full of thanks to God that he led us through the valley to this happy place.

My grandfather is probably the proudest man in the kirk, for my son is to bear his name too. This very small child is to be called Gareth Ian McLean Fergusson Grant.

Idly I wonder where the old paddle steamer is and if Rat knows that we have used his name without his permission. At least, he will know that Suzy will be on her way to him very soon. He will see to it, that she forgets the old unhappy times, as we all must.

I should be paying attention to the prayers.

'Almighty and everlasting God, who of thy great mercy didst save Noah and his family in the ark from perishing by water . . . and also didst lead the children of Israel through the Red Sea . . . '

It was strange that they had chosen that particular prayer and presently, Gareth

Ian McLean Fergusson Grant had been received into the Church. It was time to go back to the castle and to start celebrations. Yet as we went down the aisle, my eye searched for and found the empty place on the wall, the four holes, where the screws had been.

There were so many people, who had helped me and to whom I owed a great debt. There was John Stuart and Constance . . . and John James and Alison, my father and mother and Robert McLean my great grandfather and his son, Ian, my grandfather.

There were Mother Paul from the ruined Convent and there was a faithful French priest, who signed himself 'Paul Alexandre . . . ' There was Suzy, ah, Suzy. It might be my daughter Suzy, dark and full of mischief and as yet unborn, who would imprison a cockroach in a match box in a kirk pew, for the sheer mischief of it . . .

There were so many people to repay with some honour, yet in my imagination I saw Rat Fergusson on his bridge, saw how he would look at me, with the cap tilted over his eyes, how he would throw the oily rag to me after he had extracted it from his hip pocket.

"Wipe the slate clean, Lady. You played your own part. You were the finest of them all. Do me a favour and forget the whole thing!"

But who could forget what went on? Certainly not I! And to say I was the finest of them all is a Rat Fergusson lie . . . I give you my word on it.

THE END

THE WILDERNESS WALK
Sheila Bishop

Stifling unpleasant memories of a misbegotten romance in Cleave with Lord Francis Aubrey, Lavinia goes on holiday there with her sister. The two women are thrust into a romantic intrigue involving none other than Lord Francis.

THE RELUCTANT GUEST
Rosalind Brett

Ann Calvert went to spend a month on a South African farm with Theo Borland and his sister. They both proved to be different from her first idea of them, and there was Storr Peterson — the most disturbing man she had ever met.

ONE ENCHANTED SUMMER
Anne Tedlock Brooks

A tale of mystery and romance and a girl who found both during one enchanted summer.

CLOUD OVER MALVERTON
Nancy Buckingham

Dulcie soon realises that something is seriously wrong at Malverton, and when violence strikes she is horrified to find herself under suspicion of murder.

AFTER THOUGHTS
Max Bygraves

The Cockney entertainer tells stories of his East End childhood, of his RAF days, and his post-war showbusiness successes and friendships with fellow comedians.

MOONLIGHT
AND MARCH ROSES
D. Y. Cameron

Lynn's search to trace a missing girl takes her to Spain, where she meets Clive Hendon. While untangling the situation, she untangles her emotions and decides on her own future.

NURSE ALICE IN LOVE
Theresa Charles

Accepting the post of nurse to little Fernie Sherrod, Alice Everton could not guess at the romance, suspense and danger which lay ahead at the Sherrod's isolated estate.

POIROT INVESTIGATES
Agatha Christie

Two things bind these eleven stories together — the brilliance and uncanny skill of the diminutive Belgian detective, and the stupidity of his Watson-like partner, Captain Hastings.

LET LOOSE THE TIGERS
Josephine Cox

Queenie promised to find the long-lost son of the frail, elderly murderess, Hannah Jason. But her enquiries threatened to unlock the cage where crucial secrets had long been held captive.

THE TWILIGHT MAN
Frank Gruber

Jim Rand lives alone in the California desert awaiting death. Into his hermit existence comes a teenage girl who blows both his past and his brief future wide open.

DOG IN THE DARK
Gerald Hammond

Jim Cunningham breeds and trains gun dogs, and his antagonism towards the devotees of show spaniels earns him many enemies. So when one of them is found murdered, the police are on his doorstep within hours.

THE RED KNIGHT
Geoffrey Moxon

When he finds himself a pawn on the chessboard of international espionage with his family in constant danger, Guy Trent becomes embroiled in moves and countermoves which may mean life or death for Western scientists.

TIGER TIGER
Frank Ryan

A young man involved in drugs is found murdered. This is the first event which will draw Detective Inspector Sandy Woodings into a whirlpool of murder and deceit.

CAROLINE MINUSCULE
Andrew Taylor

Caroline Minuscule, a medieval script, is the first clue to the whereabouts of a cache of diamonds. The search becomes a deadly kind of fairy story in which several murders have an other-worldly quality.

LONG CHAIN OF DEATH
Sarah Wolf

During the Second World War four American teenagers from the same town join the Army together. Forty-two years later, the son of one of the soldiers realises that someone is systematically wiping out the families of the four men.